# Doodles Lanhorn
## and the Quest to Save Inner Earth

"Russell D. Bernstein's novel, *Doodles Lanhorn and the Quest to Save Inner Earth*, is a modern day fable of an innovative boy using his creativity to develop strategies to successfully defeat bullying."

—Paula Fradiani Ed.D., Child Advocate

Published by:
Hannacroix Creek Books, Inc.
1127 High Ridge Road, #110
Stamford, CT 06905 USA
http://www.hannacroixcreekbooks.com
hannacroix@aol.com
Follow us on Twitter: @hannacroixcreek

Library of Congress Control Number: 2015960905

ISBN: 978-1-938998-40-9 (trade paperback)

# Doodles Lanhorn

## and the Quest to Save Inner Earth

Russell D. Bernstein

Hannacroix Creek Books, Inc.
Stamford, Connecticut

Other Novels by Russell D. Bernstein

*Doodles: When Art and Magic Collide* (2014)

## Dedication

To all those who believed in me, I tip my Wizartry hat to you and to all those who did not believe in me, there is no such thing as Wizartry.

A special thank you to Helena Davison who is a great Wizart and an even greater friend.

## Chapter 1

**N**ighttime came early despite it being summer. An eerie quiet had settled over Hollyport, a small town in northern Idaho, nestled against Lake Ono Pala. The gentle, rhythmic sound of waves crashing against the piers in Dockside, the fish market side of town, the soft chirping of birds in their carefully made nests in the parks, the gentle breeze prickling the tops of freshly mowed lawns and rustling the lush green leaves on the trees were the only sounds in the night air. Suddenly, without warning, there was a loud *boom!* It sounded like an explosion and it rattled adjacent building windows, setting off car alarms all along the street. The source most certainly emanated from within a building as there was a loud, yet muffled rumbling. It sounded like thunder, only thunder does not occur indoors.

Gary, the lone guard on duty in the town's largest bank, Hollyport Sovereignty, woke from his nap with a start. He tripped over his untied shoes and fell to the floor. As he stood up, the ground trembled violently, threatening to topple him onto the floor again.

"No, no, no!"

He reached for his keys as he hastily retied his shoes and proceeded to run toward the steel vault. His hands were shaking so much that he had trouble hanging on to the keys as he ran.

1

Gary had promised that he wouldn't fall asleep on duty ever again after his supervisor had done a random spot check last month. It was just so quiet and dark in here. Who could blame him for resting his eyes?

Gary turned the last corner and came to a screeching halt. The vault door, which was built as thick as a tree trunk, had a hole the size of a small car right through its center. Inside, a lanky man and a young woman stuffed money into burlap sacks. They each wore strangely elaborate, brightly colored hats, which seemed to Gary to be an odd choice of apparel for robbers to wear during a heist. The hats did nothing to cover their faces and in fact, brought even more attention to their faces. The taller man had long, curly black hair that fell down to his shoulders, steely looking blue eyes and a particularly angular face. He wore a well-fitted, black dress shirt and dark grey suit pants; his black dress shoes were shined to immaculate perfection. The woman was short and muscular. She had a fierce look about her and her movements were quick and deliberate; her chin jutted outward in a permanent challenge to anyone who crossed her path. Her dark brown eyes had a fiery determination in them.

Gary reached for his weapon, but the tall man heard him and turned sharply around, pointing a large crossbow at the would-be hero.

"I wouldn't do that, if I were you." The man's voice was deep, calm and confident. Either they were professionals or this was a fearless man. Either choice did not bode well.

Gary carefully put down his weapon and held up his hands.

"Good choice," the man said.

The woman hadn't looked up the entire time. Apparently a guard's presence didn't faze her. She finished stuffing the bags with money and tapped the tall man on the shoulder. "We're good. Let's go, Alanso."

The man smiled and backed away towards a door, keeping his weapon pointed at Gary. Gary could have sworn there was no door in the back vault before, aside from the steel one at the front of the vault where he entered. That was now blown apart. What was going on? Gary was in a state of shock, his knees trembling in fear. Unfortunately, there was nothing Gary could do. He had a family who needed him. His beautiful wife and amazing two young daughters counted on him. They were his everything.

The tall man, who the woman had called Alanso, tipped his hat. "Been a pleasure." He smiled one last time and then both he and the woman were gone through the door, into the night.

Gary was left standing there, still shaking. "This is not good."

# Chapter 2

Inner Earth, a world within a world and a testing ground for aspiring Wizarts and home to those who had finally hung up their paint brushes, was at peace again. Inner Earth lay deep within the crust of Earth, a secret landscape only known by Wizarts and protected from the outside world. It was a beautiful landscape, full of magical creatures, strange and beautiful plant life and colors unique to its environment. After a recent attempt by a powerful Wizart to destroy everything, Inner Earth remained intact because of the valiant actions of a thirteen-year-old aspiring Wizart named Doodles Lanhorn. There were still remnants of decay here and there, but nothing that a little paint and the talents of the Wizarts couldn't fix. Day and night, the Wizarts gathered, painting over what was ruined and redrawing what could not be easily repaired.

Doodles wanted to help the recovery effort, but he was still being denied full access to Inner Earth's marvelous landscape. The Wizartry Council's strict rules concerning entry seemed punitive at a time like this. After all, Doodles had proven himself by saving their world and showing he could draw without needing a paint brush as the rest of the Wizarts required. Surely this talent could be put to good use at a time like this. Doodles might only be thirteen, but he was passionate and talented. His unruly red hair, lanky frame, and awkward hand-eye coordination made him an easy target for school bullies, but after everything he had been through, Doodles thought people would see that he was braver and more capable than anyone had believed and therefore, they would value his help.

"Again!" Riddley yelled so loud that he had to stop his Wizartry hat from falling off of his head.

Doodles' thoughts were interrupted by the stern sound of Riddley's voice and with a jolt, he was brought back to reality.

These past few weeks, Riddley had been testing Doodles. Riddley's unpredictable behavior constantly challenged Doodles' quick thinking and pushed his talents to their limits.

They were in Riddley's shop, the one on Lamter Lane where this adventure had all begun. It was where Doodles had become Riddley's apprentice after finding the address and a cryptic note in the back of a beautiful book of fantastic pictures he had received from his uncle and aunt for his birthday. This shop had become a second home to Doodles. Riddley may have been advanced in years, but his movements were quick and his voice as commanding as men much younger than he. Slim and tall, he towered over Doodles. Riddley's hair was turning a wispy grey, usually hidden by his oversized Wizartry hat. A slew of paint brushes and glass bottles hung from a large brown belt at his waist. The liquids and paints jostled inside the bottles as he walked.

"Just because you're tired doesn't mean I should take it easy on you," Riddley insisted.

Doodles sighed. "It's not that. I'm just worried. Why won't the council let me help them?"

"We've been over this, Doodles. Until you pass the three tests required to become a full-fledged Wizart and don your Wizartry hat, you aren't allowed," explained Riddley. "The only reason you were permitted in last time was because of an emergency to save Inner Earth. They would have sent other Wizartry members in, but they were away at the annual Wizartry conference and delayed due to weather."

"It would only be temporary and..." Doodles began.

"Rules are rules! You are not officially a Wizart yet!" Riddley's cheeks flushed with anger as his bushy eyebrows wiggled up and down, a warning sign Doodles had come to recognize. He knew when Riddley was reaching his breaking point. Riddley's pale face flushed with annoyance. The wooden floor boards in Riddley's bookstore creaked as Doodles took a wary step backwards, unsure of what Riddley's action might be.

"Fine. I'll drop it." Doodles conceded and reluctantly took up a ready stance and began again to draw with his hands.

"Faster," Riddley chided. "I said go faster, not get reckless! You must master the art of drawing swiftly *and* accurately. You're getting sloppy!" Doodles was confused. Ridley was being so much tougher than usual.

Riddley pointed to an artist easel in the corner of the room with cans of different color paint set along the floor, brushes sticking out of each one. "Remember when we first started? Maybe we should go back to the basics. You imagine something, you paint it with your brush, you sprinkle some special ingredient from the Alaka plant on it and your drawing comes to life. That was only a few steps to master. Now, all you have to do is draw with your hands. This should be easy for you."

Doodles finally threw his arms up in exasperation. "I can't do this anymore! I just want to help. I can't focus on training. Please Riddley, can't you bend the rules just this one time?"

Riddley sighed and visibly relaxed. "I know you want to help. You have a big and generous heart. You always have. You will get your chance soon enough. I can see that your head is not into this today. Come back after school Monday."

Doodles opened his mouth to protest and then thought better of it. Instead he nodded silently and left.

Riddley was left standing by himself, shaking his head. His pale face made his frown stand out even more. Doodles was only a boy of thirteen and the perils that awaited him were far too dangerous for him to face on his own. "Oh Doodles... If only you knew what lay ahead of you."

\* \* \*

The council members were running on very little sleep. Aside from their normal every-day tasks, they also had to organize repairs and answer inquiries from all over Inner Earth about security and safety concerns.

One of their late night meetings had just adjourned. Charles, the eldest of the three council members as he was in his late seventies was, as usual, the last to leave. He was their faithful secretary and he always made sure every detail of the meetings was recorded before he left, regardless of how insignificant it seemed.

Charles finally put his pen down, blew out the last of the candles, and stood up shakily. It was getting cold and his knees always hurt when there was a chill.

"Going somewhere?" a voice spoke from the shadows. The voice was familiar, a soft, yet commanding voice with an icy edge to it.

Charles reached for his paint brush. He was old but he still had talent; even though his reactions were perhaps a little slower than in his youth, they were very much intact.

He strained his eyes in order to see into the darkness. Charles quickly painted a lantern and gasped at what he saw.

Rita stood there, paint brush pointing towards his face. Her face was lit up from the light of the lantern and Charles shivered at the intensity in her eyes.

"I would like to have a word with you," Rita said. Her arm held the paint brush pointed straight at him as she spoke. Although she was shorter than Charles, and far younger, she had a commanding presence about her. Her eyes stared with an intensity of a wild tiger on the prowl. She was confident and arrogant, a combination that Charles detested.

"I have nothing to say to you," Charles said as he turned to leave but Rita moved to block his exit. Charles noted that her clothes were dusty and had several rips in the fabric. She didn't seem to care that her hair was dirty and unwashed for quite some time.

Charles sighed, realizing that Rita was not going to move. "We thought you were dead, Rita. Doodles said that you fell off of a cliff into lava. How could anyone survive that? Surely you must realize that you betrayed your own kind. You disregarded the rules and violated the very essence of what it means to be a Wizart, and you dared to defile our land! You used the great Eraser to try to destroy Inner Earth! All the land's creations, all its wonderful creatures and plant life were corrupted and almost wiped out completely."

He was now getting over his initial surprise and he was angry. Rita had deliberately disobeyed his orders to stay out of Inner Earth. In fact, she had tried to annihilate it! She was the reason why he was getting pressure from Wizarts from all over the world to change standard security measures, security measures that had been in place and had served them well for hundreds of years. She was the reason he could not sleep - why his eyes were red, and his eyelids heavy, night after night. "How dare you show yourself here?"

He pointed his own brush at her. His hand wobbled, not from fear but because it was a difficult task to keep his raised arm steady at his age.

Rita's smile was sinister. She seemed completely unbothered by the brush he pointed at her. "I came here for a reason and I intend to follow through on it."

\* \* \*

Doodles jumped out of bed. The last few Pancake Saturdays had been boring without his aunt and uncle there. They were off helping repair Inner Earth. But today they were supposed to be back. Doodles always looked forward to Pancake Saturdays. His aunt and uncle would come over from next door and Doodles' mother would make enough pancakes to feed the entire neighborhood. Sometimes, his uncle could eat over twenty pancakes. He was a big man after all, and had an appetite like three men. He was the pie eating champion four years in a row now. His uncle was so loving toward Doodles. His aunt was loving too, but they were opposites in so many ways. Uncle Roger was a disheveled man. He was jovial, sometimes loud, and loved to make jokes. On the other hand, Aunt Martha was always dressed in the latest fashion, neat to an extreme, with the manners of a lady and posture of a drill sergeant. Doodles always marveled at how such opposites got along so well.

He slid down the stairway banister with practiced ease and landed in a run towards the kitchen.

Doodles' father and mother were already eating.

"Where is Uncle Roger? Where is Aunt Martha?" Doodles asked as he came to a halt just short of the kitchen table. Doodles knew something was wrong the moment he had stepped into the kitchen. Besides the ominous quiet, his mother's normally well put together hair was completely disheveled, and his father's eyes looked sunken and tired as if he had been up all night.

"They couldn't make it today," his mother replied.

Doodles frowned. "Well, why not?" He had been looking forward to seeing them so much. It was very disappointing.

"Uncle Roger was called back in," his father stated, putting his fork down and looking at Doodles. "Something happened, something bad." His father was normally a confident man, one of the top lawyers in the state, but his eyes were downcast when he spoke.

Doodles looked at his father and then to his mother. "What is it?" He gave them a genuinely concerned look, afraid of the answer to come.

His father and mother looked at each other, neither one wanting to speak first.

Finally, his father continued. "One of the Wizartry council members has been kidnapped."

"Which of the council members was it?" Doodles was still standing and at this news, he plopped down into his usual seat at the end of the kitchen table. Pancake Saturday was ruined.

"Council Member Charles. I have no idea why someone would do such a thing, especially in a time like this!" Doodles' father pounded the table with his fist. He had never seen his father so angry before. People in town said his father could become quite passionate, even loud in the courtroom in his role as a lawyer, but he very rarely raised his voice or got upset at home. He was stern, yet fair and Doodles found it upsetting to see his parents this distraught.

Mr. Lanhorn continued, "Charles was about to retire. This is a deplorable act! He has served honorably on the Council for decades! He has always put others before himself! If ever there was a selfless man, Charles is the example. When we find out who and why they did this, well..." He trailed off as he clenched his fist as if he were going to hit the table again. At the last second, and with great effort, he took a deep breath and relaxed somewhat.

"Who kidnapped him?" Doodles asked.

"We don't know yet," his mother answered gently. "Uncle Roger went to help. If there's anyone who can find him, it's your uncle."

It hadn't been a long time since the day Doodles had stood in front of the Wizartry Council trying to pass his first test to enter the ranks of the Wizartry Guild. Although they didn't exactly treat Doodles kindly, they represented Wizarts, and Doodles was working hard to find his place among them. Anyone who kidnapped or harmed a member of the Wizartry Council was an enemy.

"This is a serious issue, Doodles," said his father. "This is a man who holds a lot of respect amongst Wizarts." His father suddenly pointed at Doodles. "At your next lesson, I want you to ask Riddley how you can help."

"I can't," Doodles said and after seeing the look his father made, he added, "It's not that I don't want to, but Riddley says I can't have access to Inner Earth until I pass my remaining two tests."

"Wherever he is, he is not in Inner Earth. He's here. He's somewhere in our town. We would know if someone passed through the gate entranceway." Doodles' father had a distant look in his eyes as if remembering something.

Doodles gulped. "Here in Hollyport?"

His father nodded. "Roger took Boogley with him." Doodles knew Boogley enough by now to wager that Boogley had asked to come along. He always seemed up for an adventure. Doodles wasn't sure if he was a friend, a pet, or something else. After being painted and brought to life by Doodles, Boogley had gained everyone's trust by helping to save Inner Earth. He was a short, furry, wide-eyed creature with a lot of courage. He waddled when he walked and his short stubby arms made him look comical to most.

"You won't have any help this time, Doodles," his father warned. "Be careful. If you discover the whereabouts of the kidnappers, come and tell us. Don't try anything without help."

This time it was Doodles' turn to grow quiet.

# Chapter 3

Doodles had lived in Hollyport his entire life without knowing about Wizartry. Now he knew that Hollyport was the center of the Wizart world and contained the gateway to Inner Earth. It was a well-protected secret.

If the kidnappers were holding Charles here in Hollyport, it created a major problem. It meant that they could hide in plain sight and no one would know any better. Not many people knew about Wizarts. They didn't look any different from the rest of the citizens of Hollyport other than the elaborate hats they wore. The current fashion in the town was to wear nice hats and so it was sometimes quite difficult to tell Wizarts apart from non-Wizarts.

Doodles scanned the store fronts. After speaking to his father, he had decided to do some investigating of his own, walking down the streets, looking for any sign that would point him in the right direction. It was a helpless starting point, he knew, but he had no other leads.

Dockside seemed like the most logical place in town to look. Lamter Lane and Riddley's bookstore were there, as well as the gateway to Inner Earth. Even if the kidnappers weren't still here, at the very least he could try to find their trail.

Maybe Riddley could help point him in the right direction. Doodles walked quickly. The longer he took, the more he worried something really bad might happen to Charles. Charles was one of the few council members that showed him respect and acknowledged his exceptional skill set. He had been kind towards Doodles in their few meetings, and to Doodles, he represented everything good about Wizartry. The kidnappers had no right to do this.

Doodles was so lost in thought that he nearly bumped into Brandon, the school bully. Doodles looked up and gave a squeak of surprise. Brandon laughed.

"What are you doing out this late?" Brandon asked. "Isn't it past your bedtime, loser?"

Doodles frowned. He really didn't feel like dealing with a bully right now, especially with everything going on in his life.

"Just minding my own business," Doodles said with more anger than he intended. He tried to walk around Brandon, but his strong arm held him in place.

"Not so fast," Brandon said. "You giving me an attitude?"

"No. I just want to go on my way, that's all."

Doodles tried to sound calm, but he really was angry. He was angry that some kids were so cruel, angry that he felt like he couldn't do anything about it, and angry that his life was taking another unlucky turn.

"Go and draw yourself some friends, Doodles. Go on then," Brandon said, pushing Doodles on his way.

Doodles didn't wait for Brandon to change his mind. He started to jog away, afraid to look to back.

Before he knew it, Doodles stood in front of the bookstore. He gave the usual three knocks. Doodles couldn't help but think back to when he first came here. His entire life had changed in only one day. A world he never knew existed was opened up to him. Doodles had come here as a troubled boy with a boring life and few friends. He had read the hidden message in the back of the elaborately leather bound book he had received for his birthday, a book he still kept in his room and would treasure forever. At first, he had thought it was surely some type of joke- some sort of prank a person was playing on an unsuspecting reader. Nothing could have been further from the truth. The bookstore was the first place Doodles was introduced to the concept of Wizartry, and it was where he had created his first painting and brought it to life. He had grown a lot since then, had learned how to master the art of Wizartry, how to stand up for himself, how to swallow his pride and rely on his friends when he needed help, how to be confident in both his skills and his choices.

Doodles took a deep breath and knocked three times. The door swung open as it always did when he used the special knock. He stepped in and closed the door behind him.

Riddley was pacing back and forth, idly pulling at a loose thread in his hat.

"This is bad. Real bad. It's worse than the kidnapping. What are we going to do? Think Riddley. Think...," Riddley muttered to himself. His pacing quickened.

"What is it? What's wrong?" Doodles couldn't imagine anything else going on at this moment that could be worse.

Riddley exclaimed, "I got a note from the kidnappers. It claims they have Charles and will go to the media and tell the whole world about Wizartry if we don't give them what they want! We can't let that happen!"

Riddley took his hat off in frustration and threw it onto the floor.

"Why did they do this? What do they want?" Doodles asked.

Riddley shook his head in disbelief. "The only way to stop them from giving away our secrets is to formally disband the council and to allow access to Inner Earth for any person able to practice Wizartry even if they haven't passed the required three tests. Wizartry has remained a secret for thousands of years. If the rest of the world finds out about this, everyone will want to learn Wizartry, and that can't happen. People would use their learned powers to do all sorts of things, some of it foolish and some of it very bad. And, there is only a limited supply of special ingredients and Inner Earth would be overrun with scientists and governments vying for control. It would be chaos. Aside from all of that, Wizartry is a sacred art that should only be taught to those with good intent. Imagine everyone running around the streets painting whatever they wanted!"

"Well, what are we going to do?" Doodles asked.

"It's preposterous! Even if the remaining council members did as they say, there's no telling if the kidnappers will keep their end of the bargain or not. Hopefully your uncle will find the kidnappers before we have to make such a decision."

"Well, in the meantime, what can I..." Suddenly the door swung open and Boogley appeared, waddling forward on his short, stubby legs. His blue fur was covered in dirt from head to webbed feet.

"Boogley! Wait. Where have you been? Are you all right?" Doodles inquired after seeing the look on Boogley's face.

Boogley looked at Riddley and then at Doodles and shook his head slowly. Boogley's large oval eyes were downcast as he spoke. "It's your uncle! Uncle Roger has been captured too!"

\* \* \*

Riddley and Doodles looked at each other.

"What? Uncle Roger? No!" Doodles ran towards the door. Uncle Roger was the person he confided in the most, the one he could trust with all of his secrets both in the real world and with Wizartry. Sometimes Doodles found it easier to talk to Uncle

Roger than his own parents. If he ever lost him, Doodles didn't know what he would do.

"Where are you going?" Riddley called out after him.

"I have to find him!" Doodles replied as he began to open the door.

Riddley called out, "Hold on, Doodles. You don't know where you are going and you can't go on your own. If a powerful Wizart like Roger has been taken, you could be in serious danger."

Riddley started packing a small bag with brushes, dissolving ink and other various items around the store.

"You're coming along, Riddley?"

"Yes, of course I am. This isn't just some test. This is really dangerous. Too much is at stake here. Now where did I put my favorite hat?"

Boogley jumped up and down excitedly. "An adventure? Count me in too!"

Normally Doodles would have laughed at the sight of Boogley attempting to jump with his short, stubby legs but this was not a fun adventure. The secrecy of Wizartry was at stake and the lives of Uncle Roger and Charles.

"Where will we look?" Doodles asked, trying to hurry Riddley's packing along.

Boogley shook himself, dirt flying off of his fur and all over the floor.

Riddley gasped in shock. "Do that again and I will use some dissolving ink on you. Do you realize how long it takes me to keep these floors so clean?"

Boogley ignored Riddley's threat. Boogley remembered the first day Doodles had created him. There was still some resentment for having been created with short, stubby arms, but the mere fact that he was alive was a miracle, and Boogley decided to let that one slide. Come to think of it, Boogley realized he didn't like his thick fur either. Sure it was warm during the winter months, but during the summer, Hollyport was known to reach one hundred degrees or more and it made for an unbearable experience. Plus, his fur attracted every dust and dirt particle around. He was a walking mop.

Boogley finished shaking the dust off of his fur and said, "I think I know where we can start. There is an old abandoned mine at the end of town. That's why I am so dirty. Quite gross in there. I was following your uncle when all of a sudden there was a flash of light. I was blinded. When I was finally able to see, he was gone!"

"How do you know he was kidnapped? Maybe he fell down a hole. Maybe he got lost." Doodles was doubtful it was as simple as that, but hoped it was just a misinterpretation.

Boogley shook his head and Riddley gave a warning look as if to say do not get any more dirt on the floor.

"I heard a woman's voice. Someone else was there." Boogley seemed sure of it. Although Boogley was just a creature he had created, Doodles had learned to trust him. Boogley had been there through everything that had happened before when Rita had tried to destroy Inner Earth and had even saved Doodles' life once.

"What are we waiting for? Quit wasting time! Let's get going!" Riddley said as he slung a bag full of miscellaneous supplies over his shoulder.

\* \* \*

The mine was on the far side of Dockside. The waves from Lake Ono Pala crashed against the side wall of the mine, threatening to cave it in with the water's powerful waves. Doodles wondered how long the mine had been abandoned. Some of the kids at school talked about how it was haunted by ghosts.

That sounded preposterous. Although, come to think of it, after discovering Wizartry, anything was possible.

"Why did you and my uncle even come in here?" Doodles questioned. "It looks like it has been abandoned for a very long time."

Boogley kicked the ground in much the same way a kid would if he was not getting his way. "We tried to think like the kidnappers. Where would we hide if someone was looking for us?" Boogley explained. "We checked the outskirts of town by the farm, but there was no sign of anything unusual." He hopped up and down anxiously. "We have to find them. We just have to!"

"Can't we just call the police? These people were kidnapped after all." Doodles really didn't want to go into the mine. He didn't so much believe the ghost stories but it was scary all the same.

"Absolutely not!" Riddley exclaimed. "We might as well let the kidnappers go to the media. And do you know what would happen then? No, we can't let people find out about Wizartry. We must do this on our own."

Doodles sighed. He started to draw a lantern with his hands.

Riddley shook his head, his hat nearly falling off in the process. "For the life of me, I still cannot figure out how you use Wizartry without paint or a paint brush. Even so, you have a lot to learn. Starting with confidence."

He gave Doodles a nudge towards the cave opening of the mine. "Go on then," Riddley said. "Lead the way."

Doodles took a minute to look at the cave entrance. It had jagged rocks hanging down from the ceiling. It was like walking into the mouth of a dragon. The cave itself was dark. "You sure we should go in here?" Doodles asked with hesitation clear in his voice. He was not a fan of dark places.

"Doodles. You will never pass the remaining two tests without confidence. Your uncle and Charles need us. No more wasting time." Riddley motioned with his hand towards the cave.

Doodles looked down at Boogley who shrugged uncertainly. *One foot in front of the other. Almost there,* Doodles told himself. *Soon this will all be over.*

\* \* \*

Each step inside of the mine made Doodles cringe with apprehension. He imagined that at any moment the floor was going to fall out from under him. It was in situations like this that Doodles wished he didn't have such an active imagination because he could envision all sorts of terrifying scenarios in the dark. If the kidnappers were still in here, in the pitch black, Doodles was in trouble. Boogley had sharp teeth but was short and awkward. Riddley was absent-minded and unpredictable. He wasn't sure he could rely on these motley companions. He was doubtful that a furry little animal and an old man could overpower the kidnappers if they were attacked. The people they faced might be trained fighters. They would be prepared. They knew their surroundings by now. Maybe they had set traps.

"Doodles," Riddley whispered from behind.

Doodles jumped in surprise and nearly yelled out. Riddley had the uncanny ability to sneak up on him.

"Yes?" Doodles replied after regaining his composure.

"What's that on the floor?" Riddley pointed.

When Doodles shined his lantern towards where Riddley was pointing, he squinted. There was something small on the ground. Doodles carefully bent down to examine the object and after realizing what it actually was, he picked it up hurriedly. A feeling of dread ran through his body. "My uncle's paint brush. The lettering on the shaft. This is his! He would never willingly leave here without it!"

"There are footprints too. Let's see... looks like one pair of footprints heading that way," Boogley noted and then began to waddle forward while sniffing. "There is just one set but there are also drag marks. Whoever came this way left dragging something or someone," Boogley said.

"My uncle?" Doodles shoved his uncle's paint brush into his pocket. "They couldn't have gone far. Maybe we can catch them if we hurry."

Riddley smiled. "Now that's the Doodles who saved Inner Earth. Lead on then."

Doodles lifted his chin up with both resolution and anger. *I will find my uncle! I will make whoever took them wish they never set foot in Hollyport.*

# Chapter 4

Rita handed an apple to Alanso, who in turn nodded and took a huge bite out of it, not in the least concerned about the juice dribbling down his chin. He had not shaved in several days and the growing beard was starting to irritate his skin. He scratched at it vigorously.

"How much longer must we wait here, hiding like animals in this cave?" Alanso said. He stood up and peered out into the daylight of vast grassland beyond the cave opening. He had been hiding in the cave for a few days now with only Rita and her sour complaints to keep him company. This place wasn't much better than the mine they had been in a few days back.

"As soon as things fall into place." Rita was single-minded, nothing seemed to distract her from her sinister plan. She had changed in the past few weeks. She ignored the dirt that was starting to harden into her hair. The hair that wasn't covered in dirt had already begun to turn grey and her eyes were sunken- yet she maintained her determination- a fierceness in her eyes that was unwavering despite the condition of her body. "And trust me, things will fall into place." She took a look outside as well and sighed.

"Just like before?" Alanso asked. He knew it would get a rise out of her.

Rita abruptly stood up and glared at Alanso. Her eyebrows wrinkled up and her eyes narrowed. "How dare you? I underestimated Doodles. It won't happen again." She stepped closer to Alanso, and even though she was a good foot smaller, Alanso felt threatened and uncomfortable.

A few tense moments passed and ultimately Alanso shrugged and turned away. Rita made him uneasy. She was too unpredictable. He chuckled to himself, trying to alleviate the tension. "The kid has spirit. I'll give him that." He took another bite of his apple. "So what's the plan now? Are we going to sit here hidden forever? Eventually either we will wind up fighting each other or they will find us. Unlike you, I prefer to see sunlight once in a while."

Rita's look turned even sourer. "Fine," she said. "Go check to see if everything is clear outside. We take no unnecessary chances this time. Make sure no one is snooping about."

Alanso took his time with the last bite of the apple, savoring it for an unnecessary amount of time. He wasn't going to give her the satisfaction of thinking she could boss him around. Rita tapped her foot impatiently and Alanso smirked. "Why did we blow up the safe wall when we could have just left through the door we drew?"

"There are always reasons for my actions. You should know that by now. We want the cops to think it was regular burglars that pulled the job."

"But the guard... he will tell them," Alanso pointed out.

Rita laughed. "That guard is as good as fired. They will check the security feed and see him sleeping. They won't believe his crazy story, especially if there is no longer a door there. What are you still standing here for?"

Alanso pressed for more answers. "Why do we need so much money?"

Rita rolled her eyes as if it were the most obvious answer. "My plan requires money to bribe the cops. You don't need to know the specifics, only that money buys cooperation."

Alanso sighed. She still didn't trust him enough to confide every detail in him. "I feel like taking a walk," he said. He gave a theatrical bow and walked toward the cave entrance.

Rita stared after him for a few moments. "Everything will fall into place."

Hollyport was only a few miles away, nestled against the backdrop of Lake Ono Pala. The town seemed so tiny in comparison to the vastness of the surrounding grasslands and the occasional field of crops. Alanso squinted irritably against the harsh sunlight and scanned the landscape. Nothing. Why should he expect anything different than all the other times he had looked around? For days now he had kept watch, waiting for rescuers who never came. They were in the middle of nowhere. No help would come for their captives; no random wanderer would venture this far into the middle of nowhere.

Alanso was about to turn around and complain to Rita for what seemed like the millionth time about the atrocious living conditions he had to endure when he spotted something in the distance. It was too far away to make out but it was definitely moving, and fast. He took out his paint brush and began to paint. A spyglass appeared in his hands and he peered through it quickly.

It was a car, moving fast, a cloud of dust in its wake. "Rita. Someone's coming!"

Rita appeared beside him. "Let me see that!" She grabbed the spyglass from his hands. After a few moments she lowered it slowly. "It's the mayor's car."

Alanso gave Rita a concerned look. "The mayor? Are you sure?"

"Yes, I'm sure," Rita said.

He threw the core of his apple on to the grass.

"Isn't he two days early? Something must be wrong." Alanso took his brush out, suddenly aware of the possibility of trouble.

"That is the first intelligent comment you've made so far." She took her own brush out.

Alanso ignored her snide remark. He had been painstakingly ignoring her comments and demands for weeks now. He needed help to carry out the plan, and unfortunately she was the only one who could help him get what he wanted.

Rita took a few steps forward. "I told you this plan would work."

\* \* \*

The mayor gave the impression of being a warm, friendly looking man, overweight from eating at the finest restaurants in town, with a round belly, cheerful eyes coupled with dimpled cheeks that give an impression of an almost permanent smile plastered on his face. He held out a large, meaty hand and Rita shook it earnestly. Surprisingly, Rita noted the mayor had come by himself all the way out here in the grasslands. Alanso also must have thought this odd as she caught him trying to see through the tinted windows of the mayor's town car as if he expected someone else to step out.

The mayor caught his stare and his smile disappeared somewhat. "I came alone."

Rita nodded. "Do you have the documents?"

The mayor's smile returned. "Right to the point. I like that." He reached into his coat pocket and Alanso pointed his brush at the mayor.

The mayor brought out a folder. "Easy now, lad. I am the mayor after all. I don't need to carry weapons." Alanso lowered the brush in response, but kept it out anyway just in case. He was not in a trusting mood.

"These are the documents as promised. Now, about your end of the deal." The mayor was practically jumping up and down in excitement.

Rita removed the papers from inside the folder and looked them over. "These are arrest warrants for all the names I provided, correct? There are two more in the cave. You can have your men pick them up too."

"Yes, yes. Of course all of the names are on there! Even as we speak, the police are moving through streets and picking them up. I will put in a call to the chief of police to pick up the other two. Now about the other matter..." The mayor began to walk forward.

"Not so fast," Rita said. The mayor turned to look at her, with a look of surprise on his face. Alanso couldn't help notice that Rita was enjoying having all this power way too much.

"What is the problem? I held up my end of the deal. Now, show me your secrets. Teach me Wizartry. Show me Inner Earth!"

Rita smiled. "In good time, Mr. Mayor. In good time. First we need every one of those fools captured. Once behind bars, we can make a deal with the Wizartry Council to get everyone access to Inner Earth. We will make sure the council provides it in writing. You can live out your retirement there and Alanso here will teach you our tricks."

Alanso tried to hide a snort. He doubted the mayor had any real artistic talent. The man was corrupt, his friendly demeanor a front. The mayor had his hand in every illegal deal in town. Alanso wasn't sure how the mayor would justify arresting so many towns folk with no prior records, but he guessed it would involve planting evidence. It wasn't Alanso's problem.

\* \* \*

Laura idly played with her food, occasionally glancing around at the others at her table. She was in a rotten mood. She was Doodles' best friend and he hadn't had the courtesy of at least calling her to tell her where he was? It just wasn't like him to do something like that. Laura anxiously twirled her long, black hair. She had been Doodles' best friend for almost five years now and shared his interest in drawing. She had come to his defense more than once in the past when Brandon, the school bully, had tormented him. Darren sat across from her. He was bullied by Brandon and the other kids in his gang too because of his awkward lisp and his tendency to talk constantly. Today, Laura found that Darren was unusually quiet, a feat that must be no easy task for him. Anyone could tell he wanted to say something, but he somehow managed to hold back.

Laura was appreciative of the Herculean effort on Darren's part. He seemed to understand the situation. She and Darren had found a table outside of the cafeteria, away from the other kids, a place where she could think clearly, and organize her thoughts. Her mind was racing. Her heart rate was not far behind. Her best friend Doodles had been missing for days now and no one had been at his house. No one answered the phone. What was going on? Laura continued to twirl the ends of her long, black hair between her fingers, a habit she displayed when she was nervous or upset. She cared about Doodles, and she knew him well enough to know when he might be in trouble and in need of help, although sometimes he could be too stubborn to admit it. When she found him, she would let him have it.

Darren couldn't resist the urge to chime in any more. "Maybe his family went on a surprise trip."

Laura gave him a dirty look, wiping her black bangs away from her eyes so Darren could get the full effect of her stare. He didn't take the hint. He continued, despite Laura's best efforts. "I bet you he will be here tomorrow. We have a guest speaker coming in; a well-known artist. I don't think Doodles would pass up an opportunity like that."

Laura thought about it for a second. It was an almost convincing argument, but something wasn't sitting right with her. "I don't know, Darren. This just doesn't feel right. Doodles is hiding something from us. I just know it."

"What could he possibly be hiding? I mean, aside from himself?" Darren's attempt at humor fell underwhelming short of altering Laura's foul mood.

"I really think he might be in trouble." Laura leaned in across the table and whispered, "We have to look for him."

Darren shrugged. "I suppose we could try to find him, but where would we even begin to look?" Darren didn't wait for a response. "Doodles usually goes straight home after school. I know you said you checked his house, but did you look for clues?"

"Clues?" Laura rolled her eyes. "Darren, this isn't some Scooby Doo episode. This is real life. No one is going to leave a clue just lying around waiting for us."

"Maybe not. But there are no leads I can think of." Darren opened his mouth to add something else when Laura interrupted. "I suppose not but... Wait a minute! His locker!"

"What about his locker?"

"Maybe there's something in there, maybe a drawing, or a note." Laura stood up and began to sprint down the hallway. Darren hurried to catch up with her.

\* \* \*

"How are we supposed to open the locker up?" Darren pulled at the lock with all of his strength. He wasn't exactly made of muscles, but Laura knew it was a hopeless attempt for anyone's bare hands. "It won't budge," he said while catching his breath. Darren had been holding his breath as he pulled on the handle.

"Of course it won't budge, silly. That's what locks are for. You have to use the combination." Darren began to fiddle with the lock. Meanwhile, Laura tried to think about what combination of numbers Doodles might use. "Try his birthday."

"Already tried that. What about breaking it open?" Darren suggested. He tried to pull it open again. Laura laughed at Darren's stubbornness.

"Would you stop that? You can't just pull a lock off. What do you mean 'breaking in'? Aside from getting in to major trouble, I wouldn't even know where to begin."

Darren shrugged. "Maybe we could ask Brandon for help."

"Ask me for what?" a deep voice sounded behind the two of them. Darren squeaked with surprise and turned around abruptly.

Brandon, the meanest kid in the whole school, was also the strongest. He laughed. "What do you two pipsqueaks want from me?"

Darren shied away, his back now pressed against the row of lockers. If he was any skinnier he could have tried to squeeze himself into the spacing between lockers.

Brandon crossed his arms. "Well? Out with it. I don't want to waste my whole day with you two losers."

Laura bit her lip to keep calm. Unfortunately, they needed Brandon.

"We need to open Doodles' locker," she stated, trying her hardest to ignore Brandon's insult. It wouldn't do any good to have an insult contest with Brandon right now. It would be like arguing with a wall.

"Normally I would do that for fun. Seeing as you need something from his locker, might as well make you two pay for it." Brandon took a quick look down the hallway to make sure no one could overhear. "I want you to do all of my homework for a month. All of it."

"An entire month of homework just to open a locker? Are you out of your mind? That is cheating and I would never help you cheat," Laura said.

"Fine miss goody, goody, then open it yourself." Brandon began to walk away.

"Wait! Can't you just help us out?" Laura pleaded.

"What's inside that's so important anyway?" Brandon turned back to them.

Before they could say anything, Brandon removed a pocket knife from his backpack.

"What are you doing?" Laura backed away and Darren nearly fainted.

"Relax. You said you wanted me to open it, didn't you?" Brandon stuck the tip of the knife into the back hole of the lock and jiggled it around until it clicked. "There you go. Now don't say I never did anything for you." He rustled through the papers and books in Doodles' locker. "Figures. Nothing but papers and books. Nothing in here I can use. It's all yours." As Brandon walked off, Darren whispered to Laura, "That was scary."

\* \* \*

The locker was empty except for two textbooks and a larger book that was tucked into the back under a cloth.

"What is it?" Darren asked. He was too short to see into the locker. He stood on his toes and strained his neck, trying to see inside. When that didn't work he tried jumping up to peek in.

Laura grabbed the book and took it out. She quickly flipped through the pages. "Nothing. Just drawings."

"By Doodles?" Darren asked.

"No, by someone else," Laura said. She flipped through the text books, scanning for anything important or that stood out. The margins of all of Doodles' textbooks had doodles and drawings, but nothing relevant to where he was.

"Maybe we should talk to the principal. I am getting worried," said Darren. He started to pace nervously. "Or maybe we should leave a note on his front door. That way if anyone in his family comes home they can contact us and let us know everything is okay."

Laura was about to close a book of drawings when she noticed small blue lettering on the last page. She knew it was what she needed the moment she found it. "This is it. Let's go!"

"What is it? Do you know where he is?" Darren tried to see what she had found but Laura nudged him away.

"Just follow me," Laura said as she tucked the book under her arm and began to run. Darren took a deep breath and followed.

# Chapter Five

**D**oodles, Riddley, and Boogley returned to the bookstore on Lamter Lane empty handed, clothes full of dust and dirt, and exhausted. The mine turned out to be a dead end. Whoever had been there was long gone.

Quite unexpectedly, there was a knock on the door. Doodles stood up with a start.

"Are you expecting someone?" Doodles asked.

Riddley scratched his forehead. "Plenty of customers. One never knows."

Doodles gave Boogley a wary look, and edged towards the door. The knocking came again, this time louder and more urgent. He heard voices coming from the other side but couldn't make them out.

"Well, are you going to open it?" Boogley asked.

Doodles took a deep breath and opened the door.

"Doodles!" Laura wrapped Doodles in a huge embrace. "We were so worried!"

Doodles was so taken aback by the show of affection from Laura that he barely noticed Darren standing there too. "Why are you guys worried? How did you find me?"

"The book in your locker," Laura explained as she let go of Doodles and gave him a smile.

"You went in my locker? How did you even get in it?" Doodles looked back into the room to make sure Boogley was still hidden from view.

"Long story," Laura said.

"You see, in order to get in the locker, we had to..." Darren began but was interrupted by an elbow from Laura.

"Hey, what was that for?" Darren protested, but Laura had already moved on. "Where have you been? Why are you so dirty?" she asked.

Doodles ushered his friends inside and noted thankfully that Boogley had the foresight to stay hidden. If his friends saw Boogley, Doodles would be hard pressed to explain the furry creature.

Riddley just sat there, silently staring at them.

"Who is that?" Laura pointed towards Riddley who in turn tipped his Wizartry hat and nodded.

"The name is Riddley young ones," Riddley said. "I am the owner of this fine establishment."

Laura pointed at Doodles' clothes. "You are both so dirty! Doodles, what's going on?" She crossed her arms and gave that look she gave when she wouldn't budge until she had answers.

"I..." Doodles fumbled for an answer. He couldn't tell her the truth, well at least not all of it. "I... Well you see..."

"I went to your house over and over again these past few days, Doodles. No one was home. No one answered the phone. I know you, Doodles Lanhorn. I know when something isn't right."

Doodles looked towards Riddley pleadingly and Riddley shrugged. "You're on your own, Doodles. They're your friends," Riddley said. He smiled. "You can tell them. As long as you trust them to keep secrets, and I mean really trust them."

Doodles shook his head. He didn't know where to begin. He was about to share everything that he had kept hidden from his friends. He was about to open their eyes to the world of Wizartry.

He was trying to come up with the right way to tell them without making them think he was crazy. Suddenly Riddley jumped out of his chair. His eyes were open wide as he frantically looked back and forth.

"Doodles, take your friends and hide. Now!" Riddley warned.

"What? Why?" Doodles said.

"Now!" Riddley insisted.

Doodles quickly drew a box large enough for himself and his friends. Before they could ask how he did that or what was going on, Doodles ushered his friends into the box.

"I'll explain everything in a minute. Just stay quiet for now," Doodles pleaded. They huddled together under the box, his friends, each one scared and confused, looked toward Doodles.

\* \* \*

"You can't keep us locked up in these cells! You have no right!" Mr. Lanhorn gripped the iron cell bars and tried to pry them open. "We didn't do anything!"

"Yah, yah, yah, that's what everyone says," the guard said, still looking at his computer screen from his desk, a bored look on his face. "Look, the mayor explicitly put out warrants for all of your arrests." He finally looked up when Mr. Lanhorn persisted with shaking the bars. After seeing the pleading look on Aunt Martha's face, the guard shrugged. "I've got my orders. My hands are tied." He went back to typing on his computer.

Mr. Lanhorn continued. "Don't you think it's strange that none of us have prior records of committing any crimes?"

The guard didn't even bother to look up. "I don't ask questions. I just follow my orders."

"This is so frustrating!" Mrs. Lanhorn exclaimed. She turned to look back at the others. Uncle Roger sat sullenly in the corner, his arms crossed. He and his wife were the latest to be dropped off in the cell. His wife Martha paced back and forth, her usual calm and composed demeanor completely forgotten. She was a nervous wreck and did not try to hide this fact.

Riddley, who had been dragged out of the book store and been placed in the same cell as the Lanhorns, had found a small pebble on the jail cell floor and was busy tossing it up into the air. He didn't seem concerned about their predicament in the slightest. There were ten others with them.

Some of them Mrs. Lanhorn knew by name, others she only recognized from around town. All of them were Wizarts. That much she knew from Roger and Martha's introductions in the past. There was something wrong here. It was too much of a coincidence that all these law abiding citizens were suddenly in jail together, all of them with Wizartry backgrounds or ties.

Emily patted her husband on the arm. He finally let go of his grip on the bars. "Where's Doodles?" She asked.

Mr Lanhorn turned to Riddley and tried hard not to yell. "Well? You were the last one with him."

Riddley missed the pebble and let out a sigh as it fell to the floor. Distracted as usual, Riddley mumbled, "Almost two hundred catches in a row. That has to be some kind of record."

"Where is he, Riddley?" Mr. Lanhorn stamped his foot impatiently.

"Where is who?" Riddley asked.

"No games Riddley. Where is Doodles? Where is my son?" Mr. Lanhorn grabbed Riddley's arm as he started to bend down to retrieve the pebble. He put it into his pocket, removing any further distractions.

Startled into focus, Riddley frowned. "The cops came after us. I told him to hide."

"So he's safe?" Mrs. Lanhorn asked.

Riddley nodded.

"Oh, thank goodness." She wiped a tear from the corner of her eye. "Did you manage to find any clues before the police came?"

Riddley shook his head. "The police came before we had time to do any real investigating. We found Roger's brush though, some evidence of him being captured. Whoever is doing this knows exactly what they are doing."

Mr. Lanhorn handed the pebble back to Riddley who in turn smiled and proceeded to toss it into the air and catch it.

"I find it best in tense situations like this to distract yourself with something mildly entertaining," Riddley explained as he tossed the pebble into the air.

"You've been in this situation before?" Mr. Lanhorn asked.

"No, but I mean a situation when you have no control over what is happening. All we can do is wait," Riddley explained.

"My son will find us," Doodles' father stated. "He will find a way to get us out. The charges against us are false and they have no evidence against us doing anything wrong. The most they can do is hold us for twenty-four hours."

At this comment, the guard looked up. "Sorry to interrupt, but I am under strict orders to detain you until you can be fully questioned. My orders say to hold you for at least a week until a decision is reached."

"A week? A decision, about what? That's not only illegal but it's absurd! We didn't do anything!" Mr. Lanhorn grabbed the iron bars of the cell in anger and tried in vain to rip them apart. "You can't do this!"

"Not my call," the guard said and shrugged. He went back to typing on his computer.

* * *

Doodles peeked out from under the box.

"Well, can we leave yet? My leg is starting to fall asleep," Darren complained. He tried shifting to a more comfortable position but found he had barely enough room to wiggle.

"Shh. Keep it down. They could still be outside," Doodles whispered. After a few more moments passed, Doodles lifted the box up slowly. Doodles, Darren, and Laura tumbled out in a heap.

"What was that about? Why are the cops after you?" Laura asked, her hands on her hips. Laura and Darren stared at Doodles, concerned looks plastered on their young faces.

Doodles tried to come up with a proper response when Laura asked, "How did you do that? How can something you draw come to life? That's... That's impossible!" Laura backed away from the box Doodles had just drawn as if it would sprout arms and attack her at any moment. Darren scratched his head. He too gave the box a suspicious look and a wide berth.

"I know this seems strange. I didn't get a chance to explain all of this." Doodles looked from Darren to Laura, uncertain of how to proceed.

"And what exactly is all of this? Is this what you have been hiding?" Laura pressed forward. "Is this why you have been acting so strange?"

"This...this is Wizartry," Doodles explained.

"You mean Wizardry? Magic? You have been working on magic tricks?" Laura crossed her arms. "I don't buy it. That wasn't just a simple trick. What is all of this, Doodles Lanhorn?"

"Not magic tricks. It's Wizartry. The combination of art and magic, a secret I shouldn't even be sharing with you."

Darren gave a hurtful expression. "Since when do we keep secrets from each other?"

Laura chimed in, not giving Doodles a chance to think of a suitable response. "You're telling us that anything you draw can come to life? Even if that's possible, why would you keep it a secret from your best friends? I am beyond hurt, Doodles. I told you so much about my life..."

"Please. Laura...Darren... You have to understand. I wanted to tell you, but..." Doodles began.

Laura and Darren both crossed their arms, disappointment clear on their faces. "You've been keeping this secret for a long time now. You had plenty of time to tell us. And to think we were worried you were in trouble."

"I am in trouble! There are bad people after me! And now, somehow the police are after me as well," Doodles said.

Laura took a deep breath. "Doodles, we're your best friends. We want to help you, but no more secrets. Please, promise us?"

"I promise," Doodles said.

"Good." She poked Doodles in the chest. "And I hope that you keep that promise."

"There's someone I have to introduce you to before we begin." Doodles called out, "It's okay. You can come out now."

Darren and Laura looked towards each other and then took a step back as Boogley waddled forwards on his short, stubby legs. They gave a shout of surprise as Boogley approached.

"Boogley is the name. And there isn't anyone better at solving mysteries than me!" He puffed out his furry chest and lifted up his chin proudly.

"What is that? It can talk?" Darren croaked.

"Is that... Is that one of your drawings?" Laura stammered.

"Yes, don't worry. He is quite harmless," Doodles explained when he saw his friends' nervous expressions. He realized the appearance of Boogley was much more shocking than a box appearing. He would have to help his friends understand Wizartry in a way that wouldn't completely scare them.

Boogley didn't seem phased by their reactions. "Let me tell you a little bit about myself," Boogley began. "You see, it all started with a crying boy and a stinky pair of shoes..."

"Let's stay on task!" Doodles pleaded, blushing profusely. Boogley didn't seem to have a filter on him. "Where did they take Riddley?" Doodles threw the question out there so as to distract them from Boogley sharing the embarrassing story of Doodles creating Boogley during a lonely night of crying.

"I don't think it was only Riddley that the police took," Laura said. "Your parents are missing too."

"Can we check the police station?" Darren suggested.

"No!" said Doodles. "We can't go anywhere near there. They were looking for me."

"For YOU," said Laura. She stopped talking and it was clear that she was working on something. "How about this? Why don't you and Boogley stay here and lay low? They won't recognize Darren and me. We may be able to see if they're holding them there and maybe even find out what the charges are."

Doodles thought about it for a moment. "Okay, but be careful. Get in, look around, and get out as fast as you can. The last thing we need is for me to lose my best friends too. Boogley and I won't just sit here though, if that's what you're asking. We will try to see if maybe the mayor can help. My dad used to play poker with him once a month. He will help get to the bottom of this if he can. He's the mayor after all."

"Good idea," Boogley added. "Very good idea! What a team we all make!"

# Chapter 6

The mayor's house was by far the largest house in all of Hollyport. It rose above the town hall like a stalwart giant, its windows staring across the town like watchful eyes. The gardens around the house were immaculately kept, bushes cut with precision and plants that bloomed magnificently highlighted the yard.

Doodles had never been this close to the mayor's house before. His father came here for a monthly poker game. Kids weren't allowed, not that Doodles would want to sit around a boring table and pretend to be interested in cards anyhow.

Boogley had to wait at the bookstore. It was too risky walking around town. If anyone spotted Boogley, Doodles would be hard-pressed to explain his existence, let alone convince them that Boogley wouldn't try to bite them. Sure, Boogley would gnaw on the occasional table leg, but he would never hurt an actual person. The only time of year Boogley could walk around outside without having to worry was Halloween. Boogley loved his first Halloween and had made it his mission to get as much candy to eat as possible.

Before Doodles rang the doorbell, he took a deep breath. Hopefully the mayor could help untangle whatever mess his friends and family had gotten themselves into. He wondered if Laura and Darren would have any luck at the police station. He was lucky to have such caring friends. He should have confided in them earlier. Now that they knew his secret world of Wizartry, it seemed silly that he had kept it a secret from them for so long. In fact, he felt bad that he had damaged their trust in him. Even though they said they forgave him, Doodles knew it would take some time to earn back their full trust. He made a mental note to be more honest with them moving forward.

He finally rang the doorbell and waited. The door swung open mere seconds later, a rosy cheeked butler greeting him with a practiced smile.

"Hello young gentleman. How may I assist you? Mind you, we don't take solicitations."

"I need to speak to the mayor," Doodles said.

"Oh. We'll you can certainly make an appointment. You see, the mayor is a very busy man. Why don't you go down to the town hall tomorrow and make an appointment?" The butler began to close the door.

"Wait! I don't have time to wait until tomorrow. This is important!" Doodles bit back tears. He was worried about his family, but crying would not make a good impression if he wanted to be able to meet with the mayor.

"Important? I am sure it is. But no one waltzes into the mayor's own home uninvited. Rules are rules."

Doodles was so sick of hearing that. Some rules just didn't make any sense, especially some of the Wizartry council's rules. They were stubbornly outdated.

"You don't understand. This is an emergency!" Doodles pleaded.

"If it is an emergency, then by all means call the police if it can't wait until tomorrow. Otherwise, make an appointment like everyone else."

Doodles struggled to stay calm. If he wasn't even allowed to see the Mayor then how was he to ask for help.

"You don't understand. The police are the problem!" Doodles stuck his foot in the doorway so that it couldn't close. The butler gave him a dirty look.

A voice sounded from inside, "Who's making all that noise? Gerald, who's there?"

The butler turned around. "It's just a boy, sir. I informed him he should make an appointment."

The mayor came into view. "Then what is all this commotion about?" Doodles had seen the mayor on local television before, but seeing him in person made him realize why he was elected mayor. The man gave off an aura of friendliness. Even though he was clearly unused to being disturbed at home, he managed to maintain a smile. His wide eyes appeared sincere and honest.

"How can I help you, young man? You look like something is really bothering you." The mayor' smile grew as he held out his hand.

Doodles awkwardly shook the mayor's hand. "The police took all of my family and friends! They took them for no reason! I need..."

"Whoa there. Slow down," the mayor said. "First of all, come inside. This is most definitely not a topic we should be discussing outside. Come on then." The mayor waved Doodles inside.

Gerald held the door open as Doodles followed the mayor inside.

* * *

The inside was more lavishly decorated than any house Doodles had ever stepped foot in before. There were giant paintings every few feet along the high walls. Some of the paintings were abstract while others were of historical events and people. Grand statues lined the hallway and a golden-colored stairway lead up to the next floor. A massive crystal chandelier hung from the ceiling, lighting up the entire room with unnatural brightness.

"Well, I thought you said this was an emergency?" the mayor teased as he smiled knowingly. He puffed out his chest with pride. "Pretty impressive isn't it? I have always been fascinated with collecting art work." The mayor noted a painting slightly off center and adjusted it.

Doodles realized he had stopped following the mayor halfway down the hallway to admire one painting in particular. It seemed oddly familiar. Even though it was clearly meant to be abstract, it somehow reminded Doodles of Inner Earth. Doodles would have questioned this, but he had come here for a reason.

He quickened his pace to catch up to the mayor. A little further down the hallway, the mayor opened a door leading into a meeting room of some sort. There was a large, finely polished wooden table that could easily fit thirty people around it. Doodles could imagine how difficult it would be trying to hear someone from one end of the table to the other. The mayor motioned for Doodles to sit and then closed the door behind them.

When they were seated, the mayor calmly clasped his hands and smiled again. Doodles couldn't help but notice that the mayor was sweating despite the cool climate controlled temperature. In fact, if anything, it was rather cold inside.

"Now what is all this about the police?" The mayor looked genuinely concerned, but something about him was bothering Doodles. He couldn't quite put his finger on it. From Doodles' somewhat limited experience, no one was that nice all the time.

"They came and took away my family and friends. They came looking for me too!"

"Are you saying you are wanted for arrest?" The mayor's face grew suddenly dark, the smile vanishing as quickly as it had come. "Do you realize what trouble I could be in for aiding a criminal?"

"I am not a criminal!" Doodles said.

"Then why are they looking for you?" The mayor asked.

"I don't know. That's why I came to you for help. My father plays poker with you. I figured..."

"Wait. Are you Lanhorn's boy?" The mayor looked even more troubled.

"Yes. That's what I have been trying to..." Doodles stammered.

The mayor interrupted again. "You shouldn't be here."

"What do you mean?"

The mayor leaned in close. "I know who you are. I think you should leave. I can't help you."

"But you're the mayor," Doodles protested.

"I told you. I can't help you. Take it up with the police department," said the mayor.

"But if I go there they will arrest me. Then how will I get to the bottom of all of this?"

The mayor stood up. "There's nothing to get to the bottom of. The police do a fine job. I am sure there is a good reason for arresting everyone. If they are innocent, the courts will provide fair justice. Now go, please." He motioned to the door. "I have a meeting soon."

"You have to..." Doodles started.

"I don't have to do anything, young man. Let the legal system run its course. I take it you can show yourself out. Good day."

Doodles was certain that the mayor was trying to cover something up. The change in his behavior, the sweaty forehead, and the rush to get Doodles out after mentioning who he was were all suspicious.

"Please schedule an appointment next time." The mayor rushed out the door, leaving the door open and Doodles standing there alone. He waited a few seconds before exiting. The mayor was nowhere in sight. Doodles looked down the hallway which led to the front door. It was empty. He couldn't leave now. He needed answers.

Doodles crept down the hallway, heading in the opposite direction from the front door. He passed several bedrooms and offices, each one larger than his own bedroom by at least twice the size. There were fewer paintings on the walls as he got further down the hall.

He thought he could hear a muffled voice coming from behind one of the doors. He crept closer. Doodles recognized the voice as that of the mayor. He was sure of it. It sounded like he was on the phone, but he couldn't hear well enough to make out every word. Doodles began to draw with his hands.

A cup appeared in his hands. Doodles remembered that his mother used to yell at him all the time, when he was younger, for trying to listen in on his parent's arguments behind closed doors. He would put the top of a drinking glass against the wall and then put his ear against the bottom of the glass to amplify the sound. She would not be happy that he was still using this method. Doodles placed the cup against the door and listened carefully.

"No! The boy knows too much already and I have too much to lose. I kept my end of the bargain. No, I want access to Inner Earth now! You promised you would teach me. What? I have done everything you asked. No, I will not calm down! Do you know what strings I had to pull for this?"

Doodles didn't dare move as he listened. The mayor was in on some sort of deal to trade for access to Inner Earth. *How did he find out about Inner Earth? Who was the deal with? Was the deal concerning his parents or the Wizartry Council?* There were so many unanswered questions.

The mayor continued. "I gave the police the list of people to arrest. It's not my fault they couldn't find him! They will eventually. He is still in town and the town is not that large. Tomorrow? Same place? Very well. You better be there and you better keep up your end of the bargain."

Doodles heard the phone being hung up and the sound of shuffling feet. Panic set in. He quickly ran down the hallway and dove into a bedroom, crawled under a bed and held his breath. Seconds went by and then minutes. Doodles didn't dare move. He had no idea what the mayor was capable of doing if he found him.

# Chapter 7

Laura and Darren arrived at the police station out of breath. They had sprinted all the way there.

"We couldn't go home and get our bikes?" Darren complained. He gulped in some air and wiped sweat from his forehead with the back of his hand.

"We didn't have time," said Laura.

"Well we won't be any use to Doodles or his family if we fall down exhausted," Darren protested.

Laura pointed to the police station doors. "Come on. We can rest later." She practically dragged Darren up the five steps and in through the set of double doors.

The front space of the police station front waiting area was empty, except for one woman sitting there on a bench knitting. Laura stood up straight, took a deep breath to quiet her breathing and approached the front desk.

A police woman sitting behind the front desk glanced up from behind the glass window and nodded to them. "Everything okay? Can I help you, young lady?"

"No, everything is not okay, and I do hope you can help us, please. Friends of ours were arrested and we need to find out why and when they will be released," Laura stated with as much confidence as she could muster.

The police woman smiled. "One moment, let me check the prisoner list. Hmm, there are no people in our cells at the moment and from the looks of it there haven't been for a few days."

"That can't be..." Darren said from where he was standing behind Laura.

The police woman shrugged. "Sorry, we really don't have anyone on the records. I just double checked. You two look thirstier than a lizard in the desert. Let me fetch you some water. I'll be right with you Mrs. Smith." The woman knitting looked up and waved.

Before either of them could protest, the officer had disappeared through a door behind the desk area.

"Something isn't right, Laura," Darren noted.

"I know. Somehow we have to get information," Laura said.

"Maybe they had to leave for some reason. Maybe they will come back..." Darren stopped talking as the police woman returned with two cups of ice water.

"Here you go darlings. It is far too hot out there to be outside for too long," said the police woman.

She handed them the cups of water through a hole in the glass barrier that separated the work area from the public waiting room and went back to writing on a pad of yellow, legal sized paper. Another cop came in through a side door and motioned for the woman in the waiting area to follow him.

"Thank you for the water," Laura began. "You sure no one was arrested recently?"

The police woman leaned close to the glass. "I am sure no one was brought in sweetie. Hollyport doesn't see much crime these days. If your friends have been missing for at least twenty-four hours, then you can file a missing person complaint and we can look into it. It's not your parent's is it?"

"No, but my friend's family is missing," said Laura starting to get flustered.

"Here, here. No need to get yourself worked up," said the police woman. "Come on in so we can ask you some questions. More information might help us to figure out where your friend's parents might have gone. Come on then."

\* \* \*

Doodles couldn't go home. He couldn't go to the bookstore, he couldn't go to school, and he certainly couldn't go to any of his usual places either. The mayor was right. The town wasn't large enough for him to hide for long. He had to get to the bottom of this and quick. He was stuck between a rock and a hard place, although in this particular situation he was actually stuck between a bed and the mayor's floor. Not the best of situations to be sure. Doodles had thought his journey to save Inner Earth had been tough, but this was becoming increasingly difficult. With his family and the Wizartry council imprisoned, he had no one to go to for advice. Maybe Laura and Darren were having better luck, but he doubted it. Not with the way the mayor was acting.

Doodles lay on the floor under the bed trying to decide what his next move should be. Finally, when it appeared that no one had been around for a while, he found the courage to pull himself out from beneath the bed in the mayor's guest room.

Doodles knew it would not be a good idea to try to walk out the front door. By now, even if the mayor hadn't called the police, Doodles would have trouble explaining why he was still wandering about the house so long after the impromptu meeting. He snuck over to the window and tried to open it. Much to his dismay, when he moved the curtains aside he found that the window had thick iron bars on the outside. Apparently the mayor didn't think the town was as safe as he declared publicly.

Doodles began to draw the outline of a door. The outline shimmered and a simple door appeared. He opened it and walked outside, making sure to erase his drawing with some of the dissolving ink he always kept in his pocket. He made a mental note to stock up on more. His supply was running low.

Doodles was about to run off when a thought came to him. When he saved Riddley in Inner Earth, he had drawn him to stop him from falling over the edge of a chasm and into the lava below. Perhaps...no, that wouldn't work. If Riddley suddenly disappeared in front of the non Wizarts, they would discover things they shouldn't know. Riddley would never forgive Doodles for that mistake. The council surely wouldn't approve.

Doodles ran a few hundred feet to a group of trees at the outskirt of the mayor's lawn. He ducked behind one of the thicker trees, a rather wide oak, his back against its solid trunk, Doodles took the opportunity to take several deep breaths and try to calm his heart rate.

What was his next move? It was hard to think under so much stress. Where could he go that was safe? What about his family? What about the council members? How would he know where to even begin to look?

Then, as most times happened, a thought came to Doodles just as he was going to give up. He remembered the mayor's phone conversation. The mayor had said that he was going to meet with whoever was behind this tomorrow. If he could find a way to record the mayor's conversation with these people, he could prove his family's innocence for whatever bogus charges they were wrongfully accused of.

How would he follow the mayor's car though? He couldn't drive and his bike wasn't fast enough. He couldn't risk getting a taxi to follow the mayor. Where would he get a camera?

Doodles began to trace an outline of a camera, his hands moving swiftly and with purpose. A faint line of golden light appeared where his hands moved. There was a sizzling sound and the air around him shimmered brightly for a few seconds. To Doodles' dismay, a puddle of paint appeared. He tried again and again, but each time, only paint appeared. Maybe electronics were too intricate or Wizartry just wasn't able to produce them. Either way, he made a mental note to ask Riddley about it later. He needed Laura and Darren's help on this. They were his best friends and they would help him figure out what to do.

* * *

"So you're saying your friend's entire family is missing and that the police came for them?" asked Barbara, the police woman. She appeared to be rather nice, but her expression in this moment seemed dubious at best.

Laura sat next to Darren, nervously twirling her hair. "Well, not exactly."

"What do you mean 'not exactly'? Did the police come for them or not? I have no records of any search warrants or patrols in that area. No arrests," said Barbara as she leaned in close to them. "I hope this isn't a prank of some sort. You seem like nice enough kids, but wasting our time and lying to us is a crime."

Darren squeaked, "We aren't lying. We just assumed that since we saw the police come after our friend and took his...err... friend, that they took his family too. His family has been gone for a while now.

Barbara sighed. "Assuming can be a dangerous thing to do. How do you know they didn't go on vacation?"

"And leave their kid behind with no notice or anything?" Laura pointedly asked.

"I don't know about this whole police arresting thing, but if there really are people missing, we can help locate them. First off, where is your friend, Doodles? We wouldn't want him to be all alone and frightened with his family gone."

Laura and Darren looked at each other and then back to Barbara smiling at them. The clock on the wall ticked loudly in the quiet room, Laura's heartbeat quickening.

Laura gulped. "We never told you his name."

\* \* \*

Doodles headed to the police station. It was risky, but he needed to see if he could find his friends. Maybe they had discovered something useful. Maybe they had been able to clear everything up.

As he got closer, Doodles became more careful. He had learned that being reckless was a sure way to get caught. He drew himself a baseball cap and painted his hair dark black. If they had his description, it would be harder to recognize him now. Regardless of the disguise, though, Doodles was not about to waltz right into the police station, especially after how the visit to the mayor's house had gone.

The police station wasn't that big, at least compared to those in nearby towns. There wasn't much crime in Hollyport, although it seemed to Doodles that this was about to change.

Doodles kept himself out of sight across the street for some time, trying to decide if it was safe for him to go inside. Not one person had gone inside or come out of the police station since he had arrived. If Laura and Darren were still in there, it had been a few hours now. Doodles doubted there had been much of a wait time. So either they had left a while ago, or there were some really long conversations going on. Or maybe something else...

More time went by and Doodles began to wonder if there was something seriously wrong. It should not be taking this long. Doodles wished his parents had allowed him a cell phone. Laura had one. He could have called her or at least texted her. Every minute that went by was agonizing for Doodles. His strong imagination created all sorts of scary scenarios about his friends and family.

After another hour, Doodles felt that he could no longer wait. He had to find his friends. He needed their help and after all this time, if they were still inside they might need his help as well.

Doodles walked from his spot across the street and cautiously approached the side of the police building. He tried to make his strides look normal, but he felt like a hundred eyes were on him. He had a hard enough time walking the school halls. Doodles nearly stumbled as he turned clumsily into the alleyway between the police station and the public library. He looked back for a few seconds to make sure no one had followed him.

He walked along the side wall of the police building until he spotted a window with bars. It was too high up for him to look through. Doodles double checked that no one else had stepped into the alleyway and he began to draw with his hands. There was a popping noise and then a sturdy wooden ladder appeared. He leaned it against the wall, tested it to make sure it was sturdy enough to hold his weight, and climbed up.

Halfway up the ladder, Doodles peeked over the window sill and nearly fell off of the ladder. At the last second, he grabbed hold of one of the steps in a tight grip, preventing himself from a very hurtful fall to the street below. Laura and Darren were sitting on a tiny bench in the corner of a cell. They had locked them away!

He tapped on the glass. It was too thick. They didn't seem to hear him so he banged with his fist. Finally, they looked up. They jumped up off of the bench and waved to him. They were yelling something but Doodles couldn't hear what they were saying.

Doodles drew a window without bars next to the real window and opened it up. Crawling through the tight space, he hopped down into the cell, landing in an awkward pose. After catching his balance, he looked up and smiled at them.

"Doodles! You came back for us!" Laura hugged him and Darren patted him on the back.

Doodles blushed after the hug from Laura and couldn't help but notice that she was smiling at him. "We need to talk, but not here. Let me get you guys out of here first."

\* \* \*

Doodles and his friends huddled behind the rock wall of an abandoned building they knew from walking home from school. They had come here once in a while to hang out after school. It was the safest place they could think of.

"Now it all makes sense," Laura said. She threw a small rock across the pavement and watched as it skipped a few times before hitting the far wall.

Doodles looked toward her. "It does? If anything, I am more confused. Who are we supposed to trust now if we can't trust the mayor or the police?"

Darren added, "He has a point Laura. The police are in on whatever deal the mayor is involved in. Who knows where the rest of Doodles' family and friends are being kept?"

Laura held up her hand. "I know it seems confusing, but at least we know who is behind this whole thing."

Doodles shook his head. "We know one person. It takes two people to make a deal. We still don't know who was on the other end of that phone conversation."

"Good point," replied Laura. "But when we follow the mayor, he will lead us to that person."

"And then what?" asked Darren. "We're just kids. They could be dangerous."

"All we have to do is get them on camera. We stop by my house, pick up the camera, follow the mayor and then..." Laura was interrupted by Darren.

"Go to the police? Not happening. I am not risking going back there again. Not after what happened."

"No, we go to the news station. If we can get the recording of the mayor on the news, they will have no choice but to release everyone and the police will be investigated." Laura smiled. "Everything will work out."

"That's a great idea," said Doodles. "But how are we going to follow the mayor tomorrow?"

Laura frowned. They all sat quietly while she thought. Slowly she began to smile. It was clear she had an idea." We don't have to follow him if he takes us there with him."

"What?" Darren asked. "Why would he do that?"

Laura clapped excitedly. "I have an idea. Let's go get my video camera first." Doodles and Darren sat there looking at her. "Well, what are you waiting for? Let's go!"

She started to jog off and Darren and Doodles looked at each other. They shrugged and followed.

# Chapter 8

The mayor of Hollyport locked the front door and hurried to his limo. He didn't wait for his driver to open the door for him. Instead he swung the door open and jumped inside. Once seated, he poured himself a drink and wiped sweat from his brow with a linen napkin from the built-in snack bar.

"Hurry up," he called to the driver from the back seat intercom. I want to get there as soon as possible," the mayor informed the driver.

"Yes sir. Of course."

"Good," the mayor said as he shifted in his seat. These were elite limousines with the top rated comfortable seats. He had bought the company a long time ago and found it to be quite useful and lucrative. But even so, the mayor found himself constantly trying to find a comfortable position. He was worried. The longer these illegal arrests went on, the more chance he had of getting caught. Money could only persuade people for so long.

The sooner he moved to Inner Earth, the better. From what that woman Rita had described, it was a magical and beautiful place, hidden from the eyes of most of the world. It would be a perfect retirement. To be able to draw whatever he wanted and have it come to life. Imagine the possibilities!

The mayor's phone rang. He grabbed it and picked up before the second ring. "Yes, what is it?"

Doodles, Laura, and Darren all pressed their ears against the trunk wall in order to hear better. Every bump the limo went over made it very uncomfortable and difficult to hear.

"Yes, I'm on my way. This is getting too dangerous. I need to go to Inner Earth now. Everyone you asked for except that kid is in the location you requested. What? Change of plans? What do you mean? Fine."

The mayor hung up the phone and pressed an intercom button on the seat panel.

"Yes sir?" the driver's voice asked over the intercom.

"Change of plans. Take me to the corner of Elm and Washington."

Doodles gasped. That was where he had entered Inner Earth during his first test. "That's where the entrance to Inner Earth is!" he exclaimed.

* * *

The limo came to a stop. Doodles heard a door open and then slam shut. Darren was about to grab the trunk release cable, when Doodles pressed his hand down on Darren's hand.

"Not yet," Doodles cautioned. "We need to give them some time to get clear of the car so they don't see us getting out of it."

Darren moaned in protest. "We have to stop him from entering Inner Earth!"

"If this plan is going to work, we need to be patient. Remember, we need to be close enough to get the video and audio, but far enough away to not be seen," said Laura.

Darren fidgeted uncomfortably. "There's no room back here. I feel like I can't breathe. I think I'm getting claustrophobic. Is the camera battery charged?"

Laura sighed. "Yes, it's charged. We'll leave in one minute. Just be patient."

"It's so dark in here," Darren complained.

Doodles drew a flashlight with his hands and turned it on.

"I still can't get over that. It's amazing," Laura said to Doodles. "The possibilities for what you can draw are endless."

"I think we can go now," Darren pleaded.

"Okay. Really careful though." Laura nodded to Doodles who in turn drew a small door hatch in the roof of the trunk. He popped it open and crawled out. "Coast is clear."

Darren didn't hesitate. He practically fell out of the trunk, Laura right behind him. It had been a very tight fit for all three of them.

They shielded their eyes as they adjusted to the bright sun after being in the dark trunk for what must have been almost an hour. Both the mayor and the driver were long gone. The limo was parked against the curb in front of a flower shop. After Doodles' test in front of the council, he was granted permission to know the location of the gate to Inner Earth. This was it. Beneath this flower shop, in the basement, was the one entrance to Inner Earth and all its wonders.

"Did he stop for flowers?" asked Darren.

"No. This is where the entrance is to the place I was telling you about."

Darren looked unconvinced. "In a flower shop?"

Doodles shrugged. "As good a place as any I suppose. Who would guess that?"

"I guess that makes some sense," Darren replied.

Doodles said, "Remember, Darren, this is top secret information. You can't ever tell anybody about this."

Darren nodded.

Laura took out the camera from its case and turned it on. "We'll follow you Doodles. Go slow."

Doodles approached the flower shop door and opened it. Laura and Darren jumped back as it swung open. Doodles looked at them. "It's just a door to a flower shop."

They looked at each other and hesitantly followed Doodles into the shop. No one looked up when they entered. There were a few shoppers milling about, minding their own business. A tired-looking shopkeeper leaned casually at the front desk.

Doodles approached the desk and Laura and Darren followed. Laura put the camera back in its case for the time being. No sense in drawing suspicion or wasting the battery.

The flower shop was filled with an assortment of colorful and brilliantly bright flowers in full bloom. There were dandelions, roses, sunflowers, tulips, daisies, lilies, violets, petunias, orchids, and plenty of others. Some of them seemed very exotic. The labels were names Doodles didn't recognize and doubted anyone other than a flower enthusiast would have even heard of them. Doodles wished he had some spare time to try drawing some of these but nowadays it seemed like he was always so busy and now was not the right time.

The shopkeeper nodded to the three of them as they reached the counter.

"Can I help you?"

Doodles pointed to the door behind the counter and tapped three times on the counter, slowly and deliberately as required for access.

The man raised an eyebrow questioningly and leaned closer, whispering, "No paint brushes?"

"I'm Doodles Lanhorn. I don't need a brush." Doodles was careful to keep his voice down.

"I know who you are. You haven't earned your hat yet. And I don't know who these two are." The man wrinkled his nose as if holding a sneeze back. "Away with you. Your request for access is denied. Move along now." The man made a shooing motion with his hands.

Doodles pressed on. "We have to go in. It's an emergency! We need to save the council members and my family! They've been kidnapped and are in danger!"

"What are you talking about?" the man asked.

"Did some people just come through?" Doodles asked.

"Yes, some very important people just a few minutes ago. Not that that is any of your concern," the man's snobby tone was starting to irritate Doodles.

"It *is* my concern!" Doodles insisted. "The people who just went through are responsible for not only kidnapping my family and friends, but also the council members! I am the only one who knows how to stop them!"

The shopkeeper stared at Doodles. Doodles stared back, refusing to turn away.

The man finally took a deep breath. "This will be a one-time exception, only because I know what you did for Inner Earth before. But, not again, until you pass the rest of your tests. Understand?"

"Yes sir," said Doodles.

"Once you are done, come right back. No dilly-dallying," said the shopkeeper.

Doodles nodded.

"Good, because if you don't, I will personally request for you to be banned from even taking the next two tests." The shopkeeper put on a fake smile as another customer approached. Doodles and his friends hurried around the counter to the back door. The shopkeeper took one last look back at them and pointed to his eyes.

# Chapter 9

**O**nce they got to the basement, Doodles searched around until he found a trap door in the basement floor. The stairs from the basement were ancient. The staircase spiraled downward in a steep decline. Lanterns hung on the walls illuminated the room. There were cave-like paintings on the walls, depicting images throughout Wizartry history. Darren, Laura, and Doodles gripped the rail tightly as they descended into the dark. The lanterns along the walls were spread far enough to give just enough light to survive a trip on the stairs.

Doodles paused when he got to the bottom. He remembered with clarity the test he had in front of the council members. He looked up and saw outlines of the spectator stands now empty. It was a weird sensation being here without the murmuring of the crowd, the stress of the test, and the glaring stares from the council members.

Laura and Darren looked around at the chamber in awe. It was an extremely large room. There were three elaborate torches and three ivory chairs in the center of the room. The spectator stands were made of some type of birch wood. The walls were covered in a bright paint that illuminated the entire room in an eerie red glow.

"This is amazing," said Darren.

Doodles walked towards the door outline on the far wall. "You haven't seen anything yet."

Darren and Laura watched as Doodles carefully traced the outline of a door with his hand. He stepped back. The outline shimmered. A wave of green light rippled across the outline and then with a loud popping noise an actual, solid door appeared.

Darren nearly fell over in surprise. "That was awesome!"

Doodles couldn't help smiling.

\* \* \*

The three friends went through the door and descended into Inner Earth. The cave floor and walls were covered in silky moss; requiring them to move at a slower pace. It was a careful and slow-going trip. Doodles painted each of them a lantern. Inside the moss-covered and gently downward sloping cave, it was frigidly cold. From his previous trip into Inner Earth, Doodles had expected it to be cold so he had drawn a sweater for each of them. But this was far colder than the last time he had entered this realm. It was a bone chilling cold now and caused all three of them to shiver in spite of their warm apparel.

"Almost there, guys," Doodles said, trying to keep up morale.

"I thought you said it was a little cold. It's like we're walking around Antarctica in the middle of winter! You would think they would have put electricity and heaters down here by now," Darren said as he wiped his cold, runny nose with the back of his sleeve.

"Be careful here," Doodles instructed. "There is a sudden drop in about..."

"Ahh!"

"Help!"

All three slid downward, arms and legs flailing about. They tried to grab onto anything solid as a sense of panic set in, but the moss was too slippery. On they went, faster and faster, deeper and deeper, yelling at the top of their lungs.

Gradually the ground leveled out and their pace slowed. Relief washed over them as they came to a stop. They sat there for a moment in silence as they caught their breath, until Darren said, "Well, at least it's warmer down here."

Laura and Doodles burst out laughing.

"Don't worry," said Doodles. "This is just the entrance. Inner Earth is beautiful. Maybe one day we will be able to explore it together during a more relaxing time. The last time I was here it was stressful and dangerous and something tells me this time won't be any less."

As their eyes adjusted to the dim light they began to see a bright spot of light ahead. It got brighter as they moved forward and soon they had reached the end of the tunnel. Beyond them they could see hills and grasslands of emerald green spread out for miles. Laura took out her camera and was about to start filming when Doodles shouted," Wait! You can't film here."

Laura turned the camera off. "Why not?"

"Because if we're going to turn this video over to the news station, they'll be able to see the whole video. We need to get them on tape without showing too much. I won't be blamed for ruining Inner Earth's secrecy."

"But you brought us in, didn't you?" asked Laura.

"Yes, but you're my best friends and I trust you. I know you'll keep the secret safe. Besides, Riddley said I could tell you about Wizartry. When we wind up rescuing everyone, they'll be too happy to be angry."

"Look!" Darren suddenly yelled out as he pointed toward the sky. They all looked up to see a giant, orange bird the size of a rhinoceros and just as fearsome looking. It was gliding across the grasslands. It was hard to make out too many details from that far up, but it was clear from the massive shadow it cast that it wasn't any type of bird they had seen before. It let out a great screeching sound as it disappeared from view. All three of them stood still with their mouths gaping open.

"How are we going to find them?" asked Darren when he had regained his composure. "Inner Earth looks gigantic!"

Doodles squinted his eyes and shielded his eyes from the sun with his hand. Nothing was in sight. They couldn't have gone too far. We got to the flower shop just after they did."

Doodles drew a spy glass and held it up to his eye. There were beautiful waterfalls, hills that would tower over anything in Hollyport, trees of unnatural colors. These beautiful wonders made it extremely difficult to focus on the task at hand.

Doodles said his thoughts out loud for a minute, "The mayor and his driver couldn't have gone too far. The only way the mayor could have gotten in to Inner Earth was if a Wizart brought him. Who would betray us?"

"Do you see anything?" Darren asked.

"No. Wait!" Doodles held his other hand to the spyglass to steady it. "There they are. In front of a small wooded area. There are four of them. The mayor, his driver, and...no!"

"What? What's wrong?" Laura asked. "Who is it?"

Doodles dropped the spyglass on the ground. "It can't be. She's supposed to be dead. It's Rita and Alanso. The ones I told you about. She's alive and they're meeting with the mayor. Laura! See if you can zoom in with the camera and get them on film."

Laura shook her head. "Won't do any good unless we get closer to record the audio. About how far away are they?"

Doodles pointed. "Probably about two miles that way."

"Let's hurry up then!" said Laura.

* * *

The three of them came to a skidding halt just shy of a few boulders about a hundred feet from the edge of the woods. The massive boulders were the size of cars. Doodles and his friends took cover easily enough.

Laura peered around the side of the boulder. "They're still there talking, but we aren't close enough to pick up their voices on the camera."

Darren looked around quickly and ducked back behind the boulder. "How are we supposed to get closer? There isn't any cover between us and them besides these boulders. They would notice us right away."

He pressed his back tight against the side of the boulder as if he needed to make himself even less visible.

Doodles thought about it for a moment. There was only grass between them and the mayor. Darren was right. They would be spotted right away. Maybe some sort of distraction would get them closer.

"I could distract them, giving us a chance to get close enough to hear," Doodles suggested.

Laura took another look. "Good idea but we would still be out in the open. We can't exactly draw a box to hide in when they turn back around."

Darren, who had finally gotten the courage to look for more than a second, pointed suddenly. "Too late! They're leaving!"

"What?" Doodles peered out from their hiding spot. "They're going into the forest. But why?"

Laura started to move to follow them. Doodles placed a hand on her shoulder. "What?" she asked. "We have to catch up. There will be more hiding places in the forest. We can catch up with them and get them on film from much closer."

"Exactly," Doodles said. "More places for them to set a trap for us too!"

"I think you being a little paranoid." Laura said.

"No I'm not. All three of them are very devious, especially Rita. I already fell into a trap she set once before. Even though they may not know we're right behind them, they may suspect someone will come after them."

Laura replied, "Well it won't do any good just standing here. We'll just have to be extra careful."

Darren spoke up. "She's right, Doodles. We don't have a choice."

Doodles took one more look at the forest and sighed. "Into the forest then."

# Chapter 10

The trees were full of leaves in every color in the spectrum and sometimes in colors Doodles had never seen before. Some colors shifted into other hues when the light hit them.

Small animals scurried about the forest floor, climbing along the great limbs of the trees, munching on the bushes and flowers and leaves. Some animals were recognizable as rabbits and squirrels. Others were monkey-like creatures with four arms and long whiskers. They swung from tree to tree with their long arms. Birds with all sorts of colored feathers and oddly shaped beaks hopped from tree to tree and soared into the sky.

"Do you know how famous we would be if we brought back video of these animals?" Darren said as he watched a giant toad-like creature walk by on six legs.

"No. We can't. I told you this place has to be kept secret." Doodles gave his friend a look.

"I know. I'm just saying."

They continued onward, making a zig zag of a trail through the underbrush, following four sets of muddy footprints. The ground was soaked from recent rain. Their own shoes were sinking into the mud with a loud sucking noise.

"Just make sure none of the footprints deviates from the path of the others. If it does, they'll figure out that they are being followed and split up to confuse us." Doodles pushed a branch away from his face just in time to avoid walking into it.

"Where does this forest lead to?" Laura asked.

Doodles shrugged. "To be honest, I don't know. There aren't exactly any maps of this place, at least not that I have seen. And I haven't really had the opportunity to explore this place on my own. I don't even know how big Inner Earth is."

Suddenly a great shadow passed overhead. They heard a roar and they looked up. A gigantic beast loomed over them. Its body was covered in brilliant blue scales, the sun sparkling from the sheen of the iridescent surfaces. A plume of smoke came out of the creature's nostrils and its sharp fangs and claws brought shivers of fear to Darren and Laura as it started to descend towards them at a rapid pace. It was a dragon! It crashed through several trees, landing in a cloud of dust and chunks of wood. Its tail swished back and forth, knocking over even more trees.

Darren and Laura dove behind a log. When they peered over the log they saw Doodles standing there not ten feet away from the great beast.

"Doodles! Get over here!" Laura called. "What are you doing?"

"Is that...is that really a dragon?" Darren asked, shaking with fear. "Maybe he's too scared to move."

"Doodles!" Laura pleaded. "Why won't he move? It's going to eat him! We have to do something Darren!"

Darren hesitated. He was scared enough of the other kids at school let alone a dragon! "I..." He picked up a rock to throw, took another look at the dragon's teeth and claws, and thought better of it.

The dragon turned its massive head and looked directly at Doodles. Laura held her breath. The dragon's eyes sparkled with intelligence and power. There was no fear in its eyes. It knew it was the largest, fiercest creature around, with unchallenged certainty. Nothing could stand in its way, no creatures, nor trees, or even mountains. The ground trembled as the dragon shifted its weight.

"Doodles run!" Laura pleaded one last time.

Doodles smiled suddenly. Maybe Doodles was spellbound by some sort of magic emanating from the dragon, Laura thought. She strained her mind to come up with something to do that would save him and not get all of them eaten.

Before she could come up with an idea, Doodles ran forward and gripped the dragon's face in a hug. "It's so good to see you again!"

The dragon made a low chuckling sound, baring his teeth. "Doodles, what a surprise!" The dragon's voice was a deep rumble.

Laura and Darren couldn't believe their eyes as their friend stood there talking to the dragon.

"How are your teeth doing?" Doodles asked.

"Good, little one. Thanks to you. What are you doing so deep in the forest? I almost mistook you for a deer. You should be more careful. Dragons do have to eat you know."

Doodles laughed. "I'm looking for four people. Have you seen them?"

"I've seen all sorts of people," the dragon said. "The view from the sky is great. Who are these people?"

"One of them is Rita. She is the person who used the Eraser that caused all the damage here in Inner Earth."

The dragon blew a plume of smoke from its nostrils. "I thought she was dead."

"I thought so too. But she's not, and she is still up to her evil deeds. We have to stop her."

Laura and Darren finally gathered the courage to come out from behind the log. The dragon turned to face them.

"More little ones? Are these friends or foes Doodles?"

"Friends!" Doodles answered suddenly afraid the dragon might attack his friends.

"Friends of Doodles are friends of mine." The dragon tilted his head and made his best attempt at a smile. Darren took a few steps back from those sharp, pointy teeth.

* * *

"I could eat the intruders," the dragon suggested.

Doodles shifted nervously. "As tempting as that is, I don't want anyone to get hurt."

"They won't hesitate to hurt you," the dragon reminded Doodles.

Doodles nodded. "I know, but if we resort to violence that makes us just as bad as them."

"If you say so," replied the dragon. It stretched out its wings and yawned sleepily. "This is all very intriguing but you will need to excuse me now. Every couple of years I like to take a nap for a few months. You caught me on the same day I was planning on closing my eyes for a little while."

Doodles laughed. "For a little while? Months?"

"I sometime forget that you little ones don't live so long as I do. I have been around for centuries and plan on taking enough naps to be around for many more." The dragon gave a snort with its nostrils, nearly blowing them over with the warm wind he exhaled. "All this flying makes me very tired." The dragon curled his tail up and shifted into a more comfortable position. "It was really nice seeing you again Doodles. You will have to visit again sometime. If you don't need my help, I think I will rest now."

"It was great to see you again," said Doodles as they walked off, leaving the dragon comfortably curled up, with its eyes closed.

"You didn't remember to tell us you had a dragon as a friend? Doodles, sometimes you baffle me. Now I am worried that all of the noise he made will have alerted Rita and her partners to our presence," Laura said. "Now they will be even more guarded, wherever they are heading."

"Did you want to be the one to tell the dragon to be quieter? Because I didn't. He is my friend but that doesn't mean he doesn't scare me a little bit."

"Good point," Laura replied. "Do you still see their tracks?

"Barely," said Doodles. "All four sets of tracks are blurred into each other. Must be walking in single file."

Darren finally spoke. He hadn't said a word since they had left the clearing the dragon had created with its tail. "A dragon... That was really a dragon, wasn't it? This is so amazing!"

Doodles laughed. "I didn't have time to tell you everything, but when we get back I will."

"Doodles, you are like the coolest kid in school. If people only knew," said Darren.

"But no one will know, Darren. We have to keep it that way," Doodles asserted.

"I know." He sounded disappointed.

"Now shush," Doodles said. "We have to try to be quiet from here on out as we get closer to them."

* * *

As they walked, flowers, the size of golden retrievers, turned towards them. It almost felt like they were watching them as they walked by. The flowers had thick stems filled with dark liquid. The stems had balloon-like petals sprouting in all directions. The petals were translucent, allowing them to see the variety of colored fluids swirling within. Some were more filled with liquid than others. Most of the petals were so full that they looked like they were about to burst.

It was a strange sensation to think that the flowers might be intelligent enough to watch them, to be aware of who was near them. This wasn't like home. Anything was possible in Inner Earth and the laws of nature, the rules and limitations that Doodles read about in school text books didn't seem to apply.

Suddenly, the animal sounds in the forest grew louder and more frantic. They could hear animals hurrying to get away, the sounds of their screeching and chirping rising quickly and then fading into the distance.

"What's going on?" Darren whispered.

Before any of them could answer, the petals of the larger flowers began to burst, liquid of all sorts of colors came shooting out in every direction. The three of them screamed and tried to cover their faces as they ran.

"What is that? Is it poisonous?" Laura yelped as she hurried to get clear. They were all covered in the different colored liquids. Laura coughed as some got in her mouth.

When they had made it past the rest of the exploding flowers, Doodles stopped running and began to laugh.

His other two friends turned back to look at him.

"What's so funny?" Laura demanded. "We could all be poisoned!"

Doodles laughed even harder. "I wouldn't worry about that, although your parents might get mad about not being able to get the stains out of your clothing." He shook his head. "I'm pretty sure it's just paint," he explained. "They are flowers filled with paint."

Laura fixed Doodles with a stern gaze. Slowly her eyes softened and a smile appeared at the corners of her mouth. She put her hands on her hips teasingly. "Doodles Lanhorn, that was not one bit funny."

\* \* \*

The woods were huge and filled with wondrous flowers and plants, some so big and colorful that it was nearly impossible to focus on walking. Each area was like a painting in itself and the three of them fought the urge to stand still and admire the scenery. After a few more miles they came upon a statue. It was an ancient looking figure, older looking even than the Mayan Statues Doodles had read about in History class. There were vines all over it, dirt and leaves scattered about its base. It looked like no one had disturbed it in centuries. What really stood out was the size of the statue. It was of a man, taller and stronger looking than any wrestler or sports player Doodles had ever seen. Whoever had created this had to have been a master at their craft. Even with all of the vines and dirt they could see that it was done with precision and detail. It was such a lifelike replica; Doodles was glad he would never have to meet this giant of a man in person. On closer inspection, they could see that the figure's body was covered in strange blue shapes, almost like an ancient symbolic language written across its body. The head was adorned with a large crown, part of it chipped away by time and weather.

"That is something I've never seen before," Doodles said. His friends were awestruck.

"Are there people like that here?" Laura asked.

"Not that I know of," Doodles responded. "I'll have to ask Riddley about it sometime when we have more time."

Laura stepped closer to examine the base of the statue. "There's writing here, and I can read it!" She leaned even closer to get a better look at the tiny writing along the foundation of the statue. "The One True King Will Return Again." She looked back towards Doodles. "Let's hope not. That figure is scary looking."

Doodles nodded. Something about the statue unnerved him. He motioned for them to head out and they all eyed the figure as they walked past, unsure if it would suddenly spring to life.

\* \* \*

After walking a few miles past the statue, they came across a clearing, one that Doodles recognized from his last adventure into Inner Earth. Only, the clearing was much different than before. A great rushing river ran down the center, a testament to the ever changing landscape of Inner Earth. The strong current crashed against jagged rocks spread throughout.

"I'm not crossing that," Darren stated with arms crossed. He watched the water rush with relentless fury and his eyes went wide with fear.

Doodles spotted a small boat on the far shore. The group they were tailing must have used that boat to cross to the other side.

"We have to cross," Doodles said. "We don't know how far the river stretches and who knows how long it will take to go around. If it even takes a day, we may be too late to stop Rita."

Darren nodded his understanding but still looked uncertain.

"We can make it," Laura told him. "Doodles can make a boat safe enough for us to cross. Isn't that right, Doodles?" She looked toward him and Doodles smiled uncertainly.

"Yes, of course I can," Doodles replied. He wasn't confident that he could, but he didn't want to let his friends down.

Doodles remembered some fishing magazines of his father's that he used to read when he was bored in the living room on rainy days. Those were big, rigged out boats, however, and he didn't think he could draw one of those. He would copy what Rita's group had used and hope for the best.

Doodles began to draw as Darren and Laura looked at him expectantly. His hands traced the outline of a boat with precision and care. He stepped back as the drawing sprung to life. A long wooden row boat with two sets of oars appeared.

"That's what we're using? No way we can make it in that!" Darren exclaimed.

"That's what Rita's group used," Doodles pointed out. Doodles didn't bother to mention that Rita's group was made up of adults who were much stronger than they were.

"What if they never made it and only the boat washed up on shore?" Darren asked.

The thought hadn't occurred to Doodles but he couldn't let Darren's worry get in the way. "They made it. You'll have to trust me. Look, I'll draw us life jackets just in case." He drew three and they quickly put them on.

Darren took a few hesitant steps closer to the river. "I hate always being the negative one," he said. "But the life jackets won't really help much if we fall in. Look at those rapids!" Indeed, the rapids looked like they had an unnaturally strong current.

Doodles knew that the longer they waited the more nervous and less likely Darren was of coming along, so Doodles prompted, "Let's get going before it turns dark. Creatures come out at night-time here and we don't want to be standing here when they do." That was enough to get his friends moving. Darren and Laura hopped into the boat and Doodles pushed it in a few feet and jumped into the boat himself. With a jolt, the current pushed them along.

"Don't stop rowing until we are all the way across, safe on the other side," Doodles shouted over the sound of the raging river.

The boat twisted back and forth in the strong current, cold water splashing up the sides and into their faces. They gripped the oars in tight fists as they rowed. Doodles looked at his friend's faces and saw determination and strength. He admired them in this moment. Although Darren said he was afraid, look at what he was accomplishing.

Soon their arms grew tired and their soaked bodies were numb with cold. Their water logged clothes clung to their bodies with icy weight.

"We're almost across," Doodles said with clattering teeth. "Just a little furt..."

He was cut off when a giant and grossly slimy tentacle wrapped itself around Laura's waist. She gave out a shout as the tentacle pulled her into the depths of the water. Doodles searched frantically for any sign of her. Whatever that was, it had taken her under the water with little effort.

Darren and Doodles screamed her name and strained their eyes trying to catch sight of her. Suddenly, Laura emerged from further down the river, soaked and grasping for anything to grab on to. The tentacle creature, whatever it was, was nowhere in sight, but the waves threatened to take her under again despite the life vest.

"Doodles, do something!" Darren screeched. Every second brought her further and further from the boat.

"Laura, hold on!" Doodles called out. He was not going to lose his best friend. He had dragged her into this mess and he would make sure she came out of it okay.

Doodles drew a round life preserver, the kind he had seen in pictures of ocean liners, attached to a thick rope like the ones they used in gym class to climb. He tied the end of the rope to the boat's oarlock. He swung the life preserver ring around his head a few times and tossed it toward Laura. It landed on a rock jutting out of the water a few feet from her. He had to reel it back in and toss it again. This time, the ring splashed down right next to her.

She quickly grabbed a hold of it with weak hands and Doodles and Darren tugged and tugged. Slowly but surely she inched closer to the boat. As she got within reach, Doodles reached out and dragged her in. She slumped into the boat exhausted just as the boat finally came up on the opposite shore. She looked up at Doodles and said with heartfelt appreciation, "thank you." She looked like she wanted to say more but she was too cold and exhausted from trying to stay afloat.

Doodles and Darren hopped out of the boat onto the shore and dragged the boat further onto the bank. With an arm around each side, the two of them managed to bring Laura on to the shore.

"Are you okay?" Darren asked.

"I thought we lost you," Doodles said.

She gave a weak smile and rested her head on the bank. Her hair was a mess as the dirt and grass stuck to every part of her head. She was too exhausted to care.

"We can rest for a bit but first we have to get out of these wet clothes," Doodles said. Quickly, he painted a few warm wool sweaters and dry socks for the three of them. Darren and Doodles turned around so Laura could change. They all felt much better in dry clothing. He looked back toward the river and could have sworn there was a massive green shadow moving along the bottom.

Laura must have seen it too because she said, "Whatever that creature is, we need to get far away from here." She motioned for them to help her up and they were on their way again.

\* \* \*

They trudged on as the forest became denser, the trees and plants sprouting thorns and vines. Now they too were forced to walk single file. Their arms would get scratched if they veered too far from a small dirt path they were following. Mosquitos bit at their exposed skin. Strange noises sounded from all sides, their sources hidden by plants and trees.

"How far do you think they're going?" Darren asked as he swatted an abnormally large mosquito on his neck.

"Hopefully not much further," Doodles replied. "I still can't believe our own mayor would stoop so low that he would join in Rita's plot. He always seemed so nice and it looked like he really cared about Hollyport and all the people living there."

"I just hope we..." Laura suddenly let out a scream as she fell into a pit. The rest of them were following so close behind that they fell in too.

Doodles moaned as he struggled to look up. His whole body ached from the fall. Laura hit her head against a rock and nearly fainted from dizziness. Darren rubbed at dirt in his eyes and mouth. Before long, a face appeared across the opening of the pit.

"Nice to see you again, Doodles," Rita smiled.

*　*　*

Doodles was stunned from the fall and completely tangled up with Laura and Darren. In addition, he was in no position to try to draw anything to use in defense. When his eyes adjusted to the dim light of the pit he looked up. Both Alanso and Rita were pointing crossbows down into the pit directly at him and his friends. Doodles had no doubt that they would unleash their arrows without hesitation and he didn't plan on giving them an excuse.

"I find it amusing that you seem to find trouble wherever you go," Rita said, a smirk annoyingly plastered on her face. "Surprised to see me?"

"How are you still alive?" Doodles croaked, dust still caught in his throat from the fall.

Rita laughed. "A better question would be how YOU have accomplished so much and lasted this long without clumsily falling off of a cliff. Yet still, you insist on following me, choosing to make more dangerous problems for yourself."

"I have no choice. You kidnapped the council, my friends, and my family! What am I supposed to do?"

"Run away. Run away to your room and doodle away and forget your problems. That would have been much safer!" Rita whispered something to Alanso who in turn disappeared from view. Rita continued, "Why can't you people see that you are unfairly hiding Inner Earth from the rest of the world? Everyone should have access. Yet you persist in hiding it!"

Doodles raised his fist and shook it. "Is that what all this is about? First you tried to destroy Inner Earth and now your master plan is to let the whole world in? Don't you understand that this will ruin it? Governments will fight over it, scientists will run tests, and animals will be captured, not to mention the whole world, not just Inner Earth, will be changed permanently. People will run around drawing whatever they want. It will be anarchy!"

"Is that what they told you?

"What do you mean?" Doodles asked.

"Everything the council tells you are lies. There is so much you don't know, Doodles. Inner Earth is where mankind all began. Everyone was a Wizart in the beginning. There were no restrictions. Everything was perfectly fine. That's the history they don't want you to know about. That's the truth."

"Even if that is true, why would they keep that a secret?" Doodles asked.

"The council formed ages ago during the first few hundred years of Inner Earth's history. They weren't content with how crowded things were getting and how everyone was equal to their stature. They wanted more space and more power. They wanted only a select few to wield the power of Wizartry. At the time, Outer Earth, or the place you call home, was a harsh and unforgiving landscape. Nobody wanted to live there. The council grew in power and formed a devoted army. Over time, they hatched a devious plan. The council banished thousands of the weaker Wizarts to Outer Earth. For a short time, those that were banished kept practicing Wizartry, making life more livable. Eventually supplies ran out and the craft was forgotten altogether. Now, those few in Inner Earth keep it secret so they may keep the control all to themselves. They decide who and how many may enter. Who are they to name themselves the gatekeepers? Who are they to deny everyone else's birthright? It's not right! It's not fair and I plan on changing that!"

"By kidnapping? How does that make it better?" Doodles coughed and shuddered as he grabbed his bruised ribs.

"No one has been killed… yet. Do you really think they won't do something to you, Doodles Lanhorn? You who can draw without any supplies, you who can change everything they have worked so hard for! Heaven forbid their master plan and long-kept secrets are ruined!"

Doodles didn't want to believe what Rita was telling him. He didn't know what to believe at this moment. Maybe she was lying. Then again, there might be some truth to what she was saying. Doodles looked up and said, "Okay, let us up and we can talk."

Rita smiled.

\* \* \*

Alanso did as Rita had instructed. He escorted the mayor and his driver, a short, stocky man named Scott, to the Wizartry palace. It is there that Rita told him to wait while she convinced Doodles to join her cause. Alanso knew better. Although Doodles was merely a kid, he would not turn against his own family and friends, no matter how convincing Rita could be.

Alanso had other plans in mind. He would continue to let Rita run things. Let her think she was in control. Besides, she did have a knack for getting things done. Then, when everything fell into place, he would act. It was all falling into place.

"Is this where I will live?" the mayor asked as they got closer to the giant entranceway. The palace made the mayor's old home seem like a doll house in comparison.

"Yes. When everything settles down," Alanso explained.

"Good. Very good. I think I will like it here," the mayor said while admiring the grand architecture and enormity of the palace.

"Yes, I would imagine so," said Alanso. "This palace was created thousands of years ago by the very best Wizarts. This palace stands as a testament to the great talent the Wizarts of ancient times possessed."

Rita's goal was to let everyone from Outer Earth in to Inner Earth. She thought it better to do it slowly. Hollyport first, several hundred people, would be her guinea pigs. Getting the mayor set up and letting him think he was in charge would make the transition for the town people easier. The townsfolk of Hollyport admired their mayor. They would listen to him, especially when they saw what Wizartry could do.

Alanso pretended to agree with Rita's plans. Her ideas were too rash, too ambitious, and Alanso didn't care about equality. He wanted power. He wanted to be king of Inner Earth and rule an army of his own. Once they fooled the mayor into working for them and the townsfolk migrated over, he would get rid of her. With her gone, he could use the mayor as a puppet and...

"Why are you smiling so much?" the mayor asked Alanso as they walked underneath stone arches fifty feet above their heads.

Alanso pretended to enjoy the view of the palace. "Been a while since I have been here," Alanso replied. "Beautiful isn't it?"

* * *

Laura and Darren sat next to Doodles on chairs that he drew for them. Rita sat opposite them. It was an awkward situation for Doodles. He didn't trust her, but at the same time, he really didn't know much about the history of Wizartry. It was possible she was telling the truth.

"I just want to talk," Rita said.

"Then let's talk," Doodles replied.

Rita nodded. "I know you don't trust me, but if what I said is true, would you agree with me? Don't you think everyone deserves to know about Inner Earth?"

Doodles thought about her question for a minute. "You tried to kill me last time we met."

"I knew you would get out eventually," Rita explained. "I spotted the calling coin in your pocket. I just needed you tied up until the spell was complete."

Doodles shook his head. "Even so, you tried to destroy Inner Earth. Now you're saying you want the entire planet to be allowed in. Sounds like you don't know what you want."

Rita's eyes narrowed. "I admit I was upset. I let it cloud my judgement. Destroying Inner Earth would not have solved anything. I realize that now. It would have made things much worse. At the time, I figured that if everyone couldn't have access, then why should just the council have control? But now there is a way. Doodles, with your help, we could let everyone in. We could work together. Think about how much we could accomplish."

Doodles scratched his head. He was really confused as conflicting emotions bounced around in his head. Everything he thought he knew was turned upside down. Maybe Rita was right. Maybe everyone should be allowed access. The council didn't have the right to withhold this knowledge from the world, did they?

"What if people abused their newly discovered powers?" Doodles asked. "What if they ran around Outer Earth robbing banks and disobeying the law? What then?" Doodles shook his head. "I don't think it is as simple as you are making it sound. There's a reason the council doesn't let everyone know."

Rita smiled patiently. "I understand your concerns, but should we just turn a blind eye because it might be difficult? Sure the initial transition might be tough, but that is why I am starting with just Hollyport. If it doesn't work, we can stop there."

Laura tapped Doodles on the shoulder. "Doodles, I don't know about all this. Imagine if people like Brandon got this power. You think he is bad now..."

Rita glared at Laura. "We will have strict laws to sway people from abusing their privilege."

Doodles stood up. "Rita. I finally understand where all of your hate is coming from. I get it. You feel the council betrayed its own kind and is wrongfully controlling who has access to Inner Earth. But I just don't think your plan will work. You need to have the mayor let my family and friends go."

Rita strained to compose herself. "I'll tell you what. I will have the mayor let your friends and family go if you promise to think about helping me. I want your word that you will at least seriously think it over. In two days, you will give me your decision. But know that if you side against me I will consider you my enemy. This is a one-time only deal."

Doodles looked to his friends and then back to Rita. "I promise I will consider your offer. Now let them go."

* * *

"You're not seriously considering siding with her, are you?" Darren asked as the three of them walked back through the forest towards the gateway to Inner Earth.

"What choice do I have? At least she will let my family and friends out," said Doodles.

The forest grew dark as the sun began to set. The darkness brought strange animal sounds, nocturnal creatures stirring. Beady red eyes stared at them from tree limbs, waiting, watching. They quickened their pace.

"I know why you agreed," said Darren. "You want to make sure you save your family. I get it. But I want to know if you are really considering her offer to betray the council and let everyone into Inner Earth. I think that's a terrible idea."

Laura added, "I agree Doodles. We trust your judgment, but this feels all wrong."

"Rita had some good points," Doodles replied.

"She is insane! She wants you to think she makes sense," Laura said as she held up her hands. "I can't believe you actually listened to her!"

"I'm not saying I will agree to work with her, but what she told me makes me realize that the council may be just as much liars as she is," said Doodles.

He kicked a rock and watched as it startled a three-eared rabbit who hopped away into the undergrowth. All of this secrecy bothered Doodles greatly. *Why didn't my own family tell me all of this? Why didn't Riddley tell me why Rita was so angry at the council? I will have to confront them. I need answers.*

# Chapter 11

"At one time the palace throne room was used as the great meeting hall of the Wizartry Council," Alanso said. "You should feel honored to be allowed to set foot in it." Alanso tapped the marble tiles with his boots, grinning as the sound echoed throughout the chamber. "As you can hear, the room was engineered to carry sound so that anyone in attendance could hear what was being said from anywhere in the room."

The mayor nodded as he approached a dais, raised high above the other seats. On it stood a throne made of silver, with intricate carvings along its exterior sides; up the arms and extending on up the back rest. The carvings depicted the palace's history, from its construction to present day, with all important Wizartry Council meetings and celebrations.

"Ah, the throne," Alanso said. "Go ahead. Sit in it. See how it feels."

The mayor took a few hesitant steps and then plopped down onto the throne. A great smile appeared on his face. "I could get used to this," he said.

"Indeed," said Alanso. "It is a wonderful palace, isn't it? This room used to be filled from wall to wall with spectators during the weekly council meetings. Guards in silver armor lined the walls. It was quite a sight from what the history books tell us."

"How long did it take to draw this place?" the mayor asked. His driver, Scott, was busy admiring the great tapestries hung on the wall. There were portraits of elderly stately men and women wearing robes and elaborate hats. The borders of the tapestries were woven with care, tiny delicate patterns expertly designed and glowing with silken threads in various jewel tone colors.

Alanso waved his arms. "The entire palace took nearly twenty years to draw. The greatest Wizarts in all of Inner Earth worked tirelessly on each intricate detail. Some of them are immortalized in the tapestries you see before you and in the dozens of statues that line the great halls."

The mayor began fidgeting in the throne. "This wasn't exactly made for comfort, was it?"

Alanso smiled. "That can be adjusted. I want you to feel comfortable in your new home. Here." Alanso quickly drew an elegant crown made of gold. He handed it to the mayor.

"A king should have a crown. Try it on," urged Alanso.

The mayor placed the crown on his head and turned to Scott. "What do you think, does it suit me?"

"Excellent, Sir. You look like a king."

The mayor nodded. "Exactly my thoughts."

*　*　*

Doodles re-read the address Rita had written down. "This is it." He looked up at the building. It was a three story dilapidated office building with rows of dusty windows. There were graffiti around the base of the front wall. Doodles couldn't help but notice that the place was in desperate need of a paint job. Even the numbers for the address threatened to fall off the wall at any moment.

"What if this is a trap?" Laura said. "You said it yourself. Rita is fond of traps."

Doodles didn't disagree with her. "We don't have a choice. We need to free them, trap or no trap."

Laura nodded. "Darren, stay out here just in case..."

"No way I'm staying out here by myself. I'm coming too," Darren said.

"Fine, but be careful. If all of us get caught, there won't be anyone left to save us," Laura said.

Laura motioned for them to follow. Doodles was impressed with her confidence. His friends had adjusted to the idea of Wizartry way faster than he would have thought.

He followed them through the front door and up the two flights of stairs. The door read number three-hundred twenty-five. Doodles held up his hand. "It's too quiet in here. Something doesn't feel right about this."

"I told you," Laura said.

Doodles knelt down and drew a peep hole in the door. When it appeared he glanced through.

"I can't see anything. Just an empty waiting room," Doodles said. He stood up and put his hand on the door knob. "We will have to go in. Get ready."

Doodles turned the door knob as slowly and as quietly as he could manage. It gave a slight creak as he pushed the door open.

Nothing jumped out at them, no one attacked them, and no traps were sprung. It was just an office waiting room. Except that it was eerily quiet. Doodles could almost hear his heartbeat.

"Hello?" Doodles called out. Listening carefully, he picked up what sounded like a response, a muffled scream coming from down the hallway. Without hesitation the three of them ran down the hallway towards the source of the sound. Doodles was the first to reach the end and he quickly opened the door, shoving it open hard enough to bang into the wall.

Riddley sat in the lone chair in an empty room, his arms tied behind his back and to the chair with rope. His mouth was covered in duct tape.

The three friends ran over and began to untie him. Darren reached over and pulled the duct tape from Riddley's mouth.

"Ouch!" screamed Riddley. "Watch it young man. That smarts." Riddley scrunched his eyes closed and put his hands over his mouth and cheeks until the burning sensation passed.

"Thank you Doodles. I knew you would find me!" Riddley said giving Darren a dirty look. "Where are the others?" Doodles asked.

"I don't know. We were separated. Rita put some sort of note in my pocket before she left." As soon as the last of the rope was untied, Riddley reached into his pocket. He took out a crumbled piece of paper and read it out loud.

*Doodles,*
*As we discussed, I am letting Riddley go as a sign of good faith that you will seriously consider my offer. I await your response at the palace at the center of Inner Earth.*
*Sincerely,*
*You know who*

"What does she mean Doodles?" Riddley asked.

"She told me she would let everyone go," Doodles replied.

Riddley took the note from Doodles' hands and read it again. "What did she mean by consider her offer? What has she been saying to you?

Doodles avoided the questions for the time being. "She must have planned this all along. She couldn't have beat us back here."

"Doodles, what did she talk to you about? What did she offer you?" Riddley pointed his finger at Doodles. "Stop avoiding the question. I may be absent-minded, but I'm not dumb, and I am most certainly not blind. I know she is up to no good."

Doodles saw no other option. Riddley could read him like a book. The man was surprisingly alert for someone who presented themselves as absent-minded. He wasn't sure how to approach the topic though. "She told me the history of Inner Earth. She told me about the exile and the secrecy. She promised to let everyone go if I agreed to consider her offer to help her open up Inner Earth to everyone, the way it was designed to be in the first place." Doodles took a deep breath and looked up at Riddley's face.

Riddley's eyes narrowed and he combed his hair back with his hand. "What exactly did she tell you?"

Doodles replied, "Everything."

Riddley took in a deep breath and let it out slowly. "We would have told you when you passed your three tests."

Doodles moaned. "So it is true? I can't believe this! You have all lied to me! What else haven't you told me? How can I trust you now?"

"Calm down," Riddley commanded. "There are good reasons for everything that was done. You are letting her get into your head. Besides, we can't change the past. You should be able to figure out the consequences if everyone is allowed to enter Inner Earth. You know why it can't be allowed. Inner Earth was only meant for a certain amount of people. If too many people are there, we would run out of the ingredients needed to perform Wizartry. The worst part would be that countries would go to war, each claiming parts of Inner Earth for themselves. They would want to study the animal and plant life there and eventually it would be destroyed. There has to be someone controlling the delicate balance we have maintained all this time. You must understand."

"Riddley, I feel like I was lied to. I shouldn't have found this out from Rita of all people."

Riddley nodded. "You're right. After you saved Inner Earth we should have realized that you are special, not like all the other candidates. We should have given you more information sooner. I am truly sorry, but it is our policy not to disclose this information until after a candidate passes their three tests, and we are strongly committed to our principles. Perhaps a little too strongly at times."

Doodles shook his head. He didn't know what to think about all of this new information.

* * *

The mayor walked the grounds of the palace, Scott hurrying to keep up with him.

"Do you trust this Alanso fellow?" the mayor asked.

"Yes, sir," Scott replied.

The mayor abruptly switched directions and Scott nearly tripped over his own feet.

"I don't know. Something about the way he is always smiling unnerves me. I didn't get to where I am today without being cautious. Then again, I also needed to take risks. Being a king would be nice, and I deserve it. Don't you think so?"

"Most decidedly so, sir."

The mayor continued to walk, speeding up and slowing down erratically. The gardens were beautiful. They were clearly painted. If not, they would have been completely overgrown by now. Since they were painted, they would never grow and would maintain their pristine looks. It was one of the many allures of Inner Earth. The mayor was too distracted at the moment to enjoy the gardens.

"Scott, I want you go back and tie up any loose ends back in Hollyport," the mayor began. "Put my house up for sale, arrange to settle any debts, close accounts." He quickened his walking pace even more. "Most importantly, gather all of my things. I will be moving here permanently. This palace in Inner Earth will be my new home. To think of all the power I will have as a king and, as a Wizart makes me excited!"

The bushes that dotted the garden paths were cut into shapes which resembled all sorts of animals, both from Outer Earth and Inner Earth. The walkways were made of stone, perfectly cut and maintained, spreading throughout the garden in winding paths. The steps leading to the lower garden grounds were made of smooth quartz, glinting majestically in the sunlight. It was undeniably beautiful.

There was a fountain made out of red stone at the center of the garden which sprayed water high into the air out of the mouth of a statue of a dragon. It was at the base of this fountain that the mayor stopped pacing. He clasped his hands behind his back and finally took the time to enjoy the view of the palace gardens.

"Yes, I think I will like it here. The first thing I will do is change some of the gardens. It is lacking a maze. I have always been fond of those and a truly grand palace should have one. And the ghastly, ancient tapestries in the throne room will have to be replaced." He took a deep breath and stretched his arms out wide.

"Yes, there will be lots of changes around here. Think of the possibilities Scott. I could make the palace even bigger. I could build a private lake with my own personal yacht. I could even build an amusement park if I want to. Changes, Scott. They are coming."

* * *

Laura and Darren waited in the back room at Riddley's shop. Doodles didn't even know there was a back room until Riddley lead them back there. Fortunately, his friends didn't mind. They understood that Doodles needed time to speak to Riddley alone.

"I know all of this is overwhelming Doodles, but please understand that this is the process. The three tests are meant to control the flow of people into Inner Earth. There is a delicate balance that must be maintained. This isn't the first time this issue has been addressed."

"I guess I understand. I was just shocked to find out this way," Doodles said.

Riddley nodded. "I understand. I am sure this isn't easy for you. If you are up to it, I have your second test."

"I am ready."

"Good," Riddley said. "Your second test is to rescue the council members and your family."

"I was planning on doing that anyway."

Riddley smiled. "Then that works out, doesn't it?"

Doodles smiled back. "I think I have figured out how to save everyone and Inner Earth."

"Care to share?"

"If my plan is going to work, no one can know what it is," Doodles replied.

Riddley gave Doodles a confused look and then nodded. "Fair enough. I trust you, and it is your quest. I will let you take the lead on this. Where are we going next?"

"After I speak to Boogley, I need to go back to Inner Earth. I need to go back by myself."

Riddley looked concerned. His eyes softened. "Please be careful. I don't need to remind you how dangerous Rita and Alanso are."

"No, I am sure they will remind me themselves," said Doodles.

Riddley laughed. "I'm glad that you're able to maintain your sense of humor through all of this."

Doodles shrugged. "You have to keep a positive attitude. Now if you will excuse me, I have to go save the council and my family. And while I'm at it, I'll save Inner Earth for the second time."

Riddley stared after him. His student had come so far in such a short period of time. He was learning to be confident and to trust his instincts.

# Chapter 12

The mayor dipped a paint brush into a jar of green paint and painted a leaf. He splashed some special ingredient on the canvas and clapped excitedly as a real leaf appeared on the ground. He picked it up and admired it, twirling it around by its stem.

"You're getting good at Wizartry," Alanso said, walking down the stone steps leading to the gardens. "Enjoying it?"

The mayor nodded. "This is amazing. With Wizartry I can do anything." He took the leaf in his meaty fist and crushed it, letting the tiny pieces fall to the ground.

Scott sipped on some tea while reclining in one of the lawn chairs. "A good show sir!"

The mayor grinned. "This is just the start. I have big plans for this place. Alanso, when is everyone coming over from Hollyport?"

"Soon," Alanso answered.

"Scott, you will leave tonight to get my things and handle my affairs?" the mayor asked.

"Of course, Sir," Scott replied.

"Alanso, this secret ingredient from the Alaka plant, how much of it is there?" the mayor asked, swirling the glass bottle containing it around in his right hand. The dark liquid splashed around.

"There is a lot, but it is not unlimited," Alanso explained. "We have to grow the plants because for some reason we can't explain, you cannot paint them."

"I see," said the mayor. "Then before everyone comes into Inner Earth, we need to stockpile as much as we can get our hands on. That way we can control the distribution and make sure we don't run out of it."

Alanso nodded. "That can be arranged. The supplies will be stored here in the palace. The palace is at the very center of Inner Earth. From here, we can oversee everything. We will be in control of the entire process as Hollyport transitions here."

"How come you don't need a canvas to create Wizartry, yet I do?" the mayor asked.

"In the beginning, each Wizart learning the craft must hone their skills with canvas," Alanso explained. "Then, as they progress, they are able to paint without use of canvas. The ancient Wizarts used to only need their hands to paint, no need for paint or paint brush. There is only one person alive today who has that skill."

"Who is it?" the mayor asked.

Alanso gave his best smile. "You need not worry about him. He is being taken care of," he said."

The mayor's normally soft eyes hardened, a look that even Alanso was startled by. "I want to know who has that power. If I am to be king, I want honest answers," the mayor demanded.

Alanso frowned. Maybe he had underestimated the mayor.

"His name is Doodles Lanhorn. He is just a boy," Alanso explained reluctantly.

"That boy was in my home the other day! Are you sure he won't be any trouble?" the mayor asked.

Alanso replied, "Rita has everything worked out. Everything is going to plan, can't you see that?"

"I see," said the mayor. "And after all of this training for me and the citizens of Hollyport, I will be declared king?" the mayor asked, his big eyes lighting up.

"Yes, unless you would prefer to be called emperor, and I will be the head of the Wizartry council. I will run the day-to-day tasks, simple things of that nature that you shouldn't be troubled with."

The mayor rubbed his hands excitedly. "Hmm, emperor, no, I think I prefer king. This is all too exciting! To think, I knew nothing about Wizartry or Inner Earth a few weeks ago."

Alanso grinned. "Yes, all very exciting."

Rita came in to view around the corner wall. She looked at the jars of paint and back to Alanso. "What's going on here?"

Alanso shrugged. "Just giving the mayor a taste of Wizartry."

Rita gave Alanso a dirty look. "Can I speak with you for a minute? Excuse us Mr. Mayor." She didn't wait for a response as she pulled Alanso by the cuff of his shirt.

"What are you doing?" Rita hissed through gritted teeth after they had moved away from the mayor. "I gave specific instructions to wait at the palace and do absolutely nothing until I returned. What about that do you not understand?"

"I had to entertain him with something. I figure we give him a little taste of what's to come; keep him happy and busy so he won't get in our way," Alanso said.

Rita stepped even closer to Alanso, her eyes locked on to his eyes. "I have everything planned out down to the smallest detail. This is not part of the plan. I don't want him getting too much power in his head too soon. What are you trying to do Alanso?" She looked at him suspiciously.

Alanso smiled. "Nothing, just wasn't thinking."

Rita poked him in the chest and kept a threatening finger directed at him. "You aren't here to think. That's my job. From now on you follow my orders exactly. No excuses. Got it?"

"Of course," Alanso replied. "You're the boss."

* * *

It was difficult for Doodles to tell Riddley and his friends to stay behind. In order for his plan to work, he had to go alone. Hopefully Boogley would follow the plan.

The forest seemed a lot darker and scarier without his friends. The animals grew bolder and even came close enough to sniff at Doodles. The foot prints were still barely visible, and led him back to the small trail. He wasn't sure if he was sweating from the heat or from his nerves being constantly on edge. Either way, he was uncomfortable and the sooner he got this done, the better. It had been some time now since he had seen his parents. He hoped they were okay and that Rita kept her word about not hurting them.

He passed the snoring dragon, still curled up within its make-shift resting place. Plumes of smoke floating out of its nostrils and creating a haze. Doodles gained more confidence knowing he had a dragon as a friend, albeit a sleeping one.

Doodles had never made it this far into the forest. According to Riddley, the ancient Wizartry palace at the heart of Inner Earth was another few miles through the woods. Riddley had told Doodles it would be impossible to miss after coming out of the tree line. Again, Doodles wished he was exploring Inner Earth under different circumstances. He would love to take his time and enjoy the scenery. Instead, he was rushing through a dark forest on his own, directly into trouble's waiting grasp.

Doodles was starting to second guess his plan. It was bold, but he had not had the time to thoroughly think out all of the possibilities. Now that he had a long walk through the forest, he had ample time to imagine all sorts of terrible outcomes. It was times like these that he wished he didn't have such a creative imagination. Doodles shook his head to rid himself of his current line of thinking. "*I have to stick to the plan. I have come this far. People are counting on me.*"

Doodles marched forward with new resolve. This was his plan, the only one he had. There was no turning back now. He kept to the trail until all of a sudden he found himself breaking through the last line of trees and out into a valley of sorts. Riddley was more than correct. The palace shot skywards, threatening to pierce through the lowest clouds. It was magnificent, like seeing a fairytale book come to life. He almost forgot what he was doing, nearly getting lost in the breathtaking beauty of the scenery before him. Doodles gave his head a little shake.

He walked forward admiring the gardens and the architecture of the area surrounding the grounds as he got closer. It was eerily quiet and empty, but Doodles could imagine it was once home to hundreds if not thousands of people. The grass was soft here, like walking on cushions. He thought about scoping out the palace first for a place to enter and then thought better of it. Better to go directly through the front door instead of sneaking around, playing games. He was done with games. If Rita wanted an answer she would have his answer face-to-face.

The drawbridge was down seemingly waiting to invite Doodles into the palace. It was made out of some type of thick reddish wood and spanned a moat filled with crystal clear water. Doodles could see giant Koi fish of all different sizes and colors swimming lazily around in the waters. He crossed the draw bridge feeling certain that he was being watched. He couldn't see anyone, but he felt eyes on him.

As soon as Doodles crossed the bridge, a figure stepped out from behind a wall. It was Rita. She smiled at him and waited as he approached.

"I assume you have had time to think about my offer?" Rita asked.

"Yes, and I can't tell you how thankful I am that you told me the truth," Doodles said. "Riddley confirmed everything that you said was true. The council lied to me."

Rita nodded. "I am happy to have shown you the truth. With your abilities, we could easily open up Inner Earth to everyone. Surely you see that now?"

Doodles nodded. "Yes. Even if it means betraying my family and friends."

Rita eyed him suspiciously. "Just like that?"

Doodles shrugged. "It's not like we would be hurting them. We are just going to change things. Besides, everyone lied to me, just like you said. You were right."

"So you will join me then?"

"Yes," Doodles answered.

Rita held her hand up and looked off towards a side wall. Alanso stepped out with a crossbow in hand and put it down on the ground.

Doodles gulped. He had no doubt now that that crossbow was meant for him if he had declined Rita's offer.

\* \* \*

Rita unfastened her belt and laid it on a wooden table. In each loophole there was a different jar of paint and several brushes.

She checked each over; tilting the bottles to see how much liquid was left in each.

"Can never be too prepared," Rita smirked as she refastened everything in its proper place. She put the belt back on.

"Where are we going?" Doodles asked.

"You and I are going to ready things for when everyone comes over."

"What about the rest of my family? Doodles asked.

Rita looked over her shoulder to make sure no one was standing about who shouldn't be. "Scott, the limo driver has already left to get the mayor's things in order. Alanso will stay behind to babysit the mayor so he doesn't get into too much trouble. As I said, your family will be released once you help see my plan through."

Doodles felt oddly unprepared with all of Rita's tools at the ready. All he needed were his hands, but it still made him feel vulnerable. "Rita, can we let my family go now?"

"As soon as everyone comes into Inner Earth and I am sure I can trust you, I will let them go." She glared at him. "And if we run into any of your friends, are you prepared to act?"

"Of course I am."

"Good. Let's go."

Doodles hesitated as she stormed out of the room. His plan had been to trick her into trusting him long enough to free his family. But it hadn't gone quite as he had hoped it would and now things were going too far. He couldn't let the world find out about Wizartry and Inner Earth, but there was not enough time to construct a new plan. He would have to think of something on the road and quick.

"Are you coming?" Rita's voice called from outside.

Doodles hurried to catch up. Obviously, Rita was too smart and careful to fall for his simple plan. So for now, he would have to keep up appearances until he could figure out a way to get her to tell him his family's location. If he stopped her now, he would never find out where his family and the council members were being held. As he followed closely behind her, Doodles noticed several papers with scribbles on them just sticking out of a pouch attached to the side of her waistband. Perhaps one of them detailed her plans, and in them, the location of his family. The only problem was that Rita would never let him read them and from the way the pouch was attached to her clothing it looked like she never took the pouch off. This was not going to be easy, but it was a hope at least, and Doodles would take anything he could get at this point.

* * *

After walking for several miles, Rita motioned for them to take a break. She sat on a log and took out a loaf of bread from a bag she carried with her. She tore it in half and tossed one end to Doodles.

"Eat it. You will need your strength," Rita said as she took a large bite out of hers.

Doodles didn't feel hungry as his stomach was full of knots from stress, but he nibbled on it anyways. The bread had gone stale and Doodles surmised that it must have been tucked in Rita's bag for several days now. Everything Rita did was so careful and calculated, everything planned out so well in advance.

"I'm not stupid," Rita suddenly said.

Doodles looked up, confused. "I never said you were."

"If you are lying to me about working with me, I will never free your family. I am the one holding all of the cards. Remember that."

Doodles didn't know what to say so he nodded and kept quiet.

After a few minutes, Rita stood up and began walking, not even waiting to see if Doodles was following. He had half a mind to stop her then and there. He could trap her and try to force her to tell him where his family was. This fleeting thought left quickly and his common sense returned. That was not the solution. She would never tell him no matter what he said or did. From what little Doodles knew of Rita, when she was set on something, nothing would stand in her way or change her mind. He would have to get his hands on those papers.

They walked in silence all the way back to the entrance to Inner Earth. She stopped before the door and looked back towards Doodles. "There will be hundreds of confused people coming through here in a few days. I will need your help to guide them back to the palace."

"I can do that," Doodles said.

"Good. And once everyone is situated, we will let your family and the council free. Who said I wasn't a fair person?" Rita said with a grin.

Doodles wanted to yell at her and tell her how crazy she sounded, but he restrained himself. It wouldn't do him any good. She was clearly out of her mind and set in her thought process.

"You will wait here to lead them while I go start the Great Migration. Catchy title, isn't it? History books will need some sort of name for this great moment in history."

Doodles had to get her to stop now. He needed to say something or do something, but he couldn't risk losing her trust and thus the chance to free his family. He would have to continue to play along until the opportunity presented itself.

She turned to leave.

"Rita," Doodles said stalling.

"What?" Rita asked, annoyed that he had interrupted her thoughts of glory.

"Maybe I should come with you?" Doodles suggested.

Rita smirked. "I appreciate the enthusiasm kid, but my plan is already thought out. You stay here." She turned to leave again.

Doodles spoke louder. "You, Alanso, and the mayor kidnapped my family and will let them go if I agree to help you right?"

She turned back sharply. "Yes! We've already been over this. Enough of your worrying. Just do your part and wait here!"

She finally left before Doodles could get the chance to say anything else.

Doodles waited a few seconds and then turned to look at the surrounding rocks. Laura and Boogley stepped out from behind them. Laura was holding her camera tightly in her hand. Doodles smiled. "Tell me you got that," Doodles said.

Laura nodded and Doodles jumped up and down in excitement. The original plan was working after all. Now all they had to do was get the tape to the news station.

# Chapter 13

Doodles and Laura ran down the streets of Hollyport. Boogley couldn't be seen in public so he had to stay behind at Riddley's shop.

"We have to make it to the news station!" Doodles called out. "Hurry!"

As they ran by shops and houses Doodles noticed that there weren't any lights on. There were closed signs in most of the windows and notices taped to each door.

"Hold up," Doodles called out. He stopped by one of the doorways and grabbed the notice that was taped to the door. It looked like someone had hastily hand written the notice with black ink.

"Look at this," Doodles said and handed her the piece of paper. "Mandatory emergency town meeting." There was some quickly scribbled information towards the bottom of the notice.

Laura didn't have to read the notice to know the address was for the mayor's house. "How did Rita get all of the notices put up and have time to get everyone to meet at the mayor's place so fast?"

Doodles read the letter again. "It says the meeting is at five tonight. She must have had someone put the notices up hours ago. Couldn't have been her. There wasn't enough time." Doodles looked at a clock through the store's window.

"It is six now! How is she always one step ahead of us?" Doodles said.

"We have to hurry!" Laura exclaimed as she began to run towards the mayor's house. Doodles followed not far behind. Hollyport was eerily quiet. It wasn't that the streets were ever truly crowded, but this was like a ghost town. Even the movie theater was closed down. Everyone in town must be at the meeting.

"Laura," Doodles said as he ran. "I know who put up the notices."

"Who?" asked Laura.

"When I was in Inner Earth, Rita mentioned that Scott, the mayor's limo driver, had already headed back to get the mayor's things. I bet you anything that Rita and Alanso gave him some other tasks as well."

"Doodles... even if we are able to stop them, Rita still has your family and the council somewhere. If we stopped them now..." Laura trailed off, not wanting to complete that thought.

Doodles was quiet for a few moments as they ran. He fought down the urge to panic. It wouldn't do anyone any good if he lost his cool now. A lot of people were counting on him. His heart was beating fast and it wasn't just from the running.

"It doesn't matter. We have to stop them," Doodles said with resolution in his voice. He sped up and this time Laura had trouble keeping up with him.

She wasn't sure that was the right decision but she would support Doodles no matter what happened. He was her best friend and there was only one Doodles Lanhorn.

* * *

The iron gates to the mayor's house were left wide open. That wasn't a good sign. Doodles and Laura ran through the gates and up the long driveway. All of the lights were on in the house.

Doodles was the first to arrive at the door and pounded his fist on it. He then pressed the doorbell over and over again.

Doodles peered through the windows. No one was inside, as far as he could see, and no sound came from the house. No rude butler greeted them at the door like last time Doodles had come here seeking the mayor's aid.

"We're too late!" Laura yelled in dismay. She kicked the base of the front door in disappointment and frustration.

"Maybe not. She may not have had time to say too much yet," said Doodles. "If we can stop them before they get to the entrance to Inner Earth we can talk to them, try to make them see how dangerous and crazy she is. She has no way to prove to them that Inner Earth is real until they see it all with their own eyes. Besides, knowing Rita, she will want some sort of grand reveal so she won't give away too many of the secrets of Inner Earth. I think we can make it in time!"

Doodles was already running before he finished his sentence. How could they possibly stop Rita when everything seemed so perfectly calculated? Who knows how far ahead she was? What if they took a different way to get there? The only option they had was to run, and run fast. Laura looked tired and defeated and Doodles wanted to give her hope.

"We're going to make it," Doodles said to her as they ran.

Doodles's legs were starting to burn and he was developing a cramp in his side from all of this running. He was never much of an athlete. He was sweating, and his breathing was erratic. He looked over to Laura who seemed to be in much better shape than he was, although even she was starting to show signs of fatigue.

Hollyport was made up of roughly eight-hundred people. Even that many people might tip the delicate balance of Inner Earth and destroy it permanently. Doodles knew he had to stop them.

The flower shop came into view. It was not a good sign that there were no people waiting outside. Eight hundred people could not fit into that shop at one time. The line of people would have stretched well around the block. They either hadn't arrived yet, or more likely took a different route to get here. It was a small and unimpressive flower shop, aptly picked as the hidden gateway into Inner Earth. No one would assume it was hiding the gateway.

Laura and Doodles opened the door by crashing into it and stumbling inside. They were going so fast that the chimes hanging on the door flew off and onto the floor with a loud crash.

The store was empty except for the shopkeeper they had met last time they were here. He was lying on the floor, a dazed expression on his face. His eyes swollen and red as if he had just cried.

Doodles ran over to him. "Are you okay?" When the shopkeeper did not respond, Doodles placed both his hands on the man's shoulders and shook him. "Hello? Are you okay, can I help you? Where is everyone?"

The man had a faraway look in his eyes as if still in shock.

"I tried to stop them," he whispered hoarsely. "There were just too many..."

Doodles looked at Laura and then to the entrance to Inner Earth. They were too late.

# Chapter 14

Deep within Inner Earth, a three-eyed rabbit's ears perked up at the sound of footsteps. It leapt over a fallen log and peeked over the top, back along the grasslands. The ground trembled and the rabbit crouched even further. In the distance, a hazy view of an army of people came into sight on the horizon, marching like humans usually do, recklessly stomping all over perfectly edible grass. It wasn't an army though; they weren't organized. Instead, they walked in smaller groups, looking at all of the sights as if they had never been to Inner Earth before.

Never before had the rabbit seen so many humans at once. *Where were they coming from? Better yet, where were they going?* The rabbit hopped and skipped along, moving stealthily from log to rock to tree, always watching, always aware of the mass of humans. Their feet tore up the grass; muddied the dirt beneath. Their sweaty smell was pungent even from this distance. The rabbit's nose wrinkled with distaste.

The crowd of humans headed into the woods, and that meant there was only one place they were headed; the ancient Wizartry palace. The rabbit nibbled quickly on a nearby plant. He would need a lot more energy if he were to run far. He let the line of humans disappear into the woods and then bounded back across the grasslands towards a group of caves several miles away.

As he got closer, the rabbit slowed and carefully walked across the cave entrance. A man appeared out of the shadows of the recesses of the cave, his body covered in blue paint, ancient words scribbled across his forearms, legs and chest. He was a powerful-looking man, his eyes hard set and his chin jutted out with assurance. His walk was that of someone confident; unafraid. He reached down with giant hands and patted the rabbit on the head, scratched behind its ears, to which the rabbit gratefully closed its eyes. He appreciated the attention.

"You bring me news?" The man's deep voice rumbled.

The rabbit nodded and pointed towards the woods and the palace beyond.

The man turned and gazed into the distance as if remembering a time long ago. "So the time has come. Thank you my furry friend." He gave the rabbit one last pat on the head and turned back towards the back of the cave. He disappeared into its depths once again and moments later returned, clutching a crown in his hands. He placed the crown on his head and stretched out his muscles. The blue writing along his body glowed faintly, emitting an aura of power.

"Time for them to be reminded who their true leader is."

* * *

The former mayor of Hollyport, now known as King of Inner Earth, stood on the top of the palace's outer wall. He clapped excitedly as he spotted the first of the newcomers appear at the edge of the forest. Alanso smiled as well. Everything was working out perfectly. Once Rita came back with everyone and everything was settled, he would get rid of her and anyone else who could stand in his way, thus setting himself up to rule Inner Earth by controlling this dolt of a king.

"They are coming," the King called out with excitement. Alanso wanted badly to point out what an obvious statement it was, but instead he chose only to nod. He needed the king to not only like him but trust him.

"You will be a fitting ruler," Alanso said. "You should greet them down by the bridge. Let them know who is king."

"Good idea." The king turned and walked off towards the stairwell leading to the ground floor. He was dressed in an absurdly long robe, the crown, a little too small, sitting squarely on his oversized head. Alanso could have made the robe shorter for him, but it was far too amusing to watch the man stumble every so often when his feet got tangled in the hem.

The stairwell wound its way in a spiral, carved with thick slabs of stone all the way to the base of the wall, ending not too far from the drawbridge. It was there that the king and Alanso waited for the citizens of Hollyport to arrive.

"They will expect you to give a speech as their new ruler. I have taken the liberty of preparing one for you," Alanso said, handing a piece of paper to the king.

"That was very thoughtful of you, Alanso. Thank you," The king said and then cleared his throat several times in order to start to rehearse the words on the paper. He paced back and forth as he did so, a habit Alanso found particularly annoying. A habit he would have to break if Alanso planned on keeping him around or else it would drive him crazy.

The column of Hollyport citizens approached. Alanso could now see some of their faces, which as expected, were turned up towards the palace walls in awe. Alanso remembered the first time he had seen the palace and was sure his face had looked much the same on that day as theirs looked now.

Alanso cleared his throat and the king looked up.

"Ah, yes of course," the king said, shuffling forward so as to not trip over his robes again.

"Remember to read the words exactly as they are written on the paper," Alanso whispered.

The king nodded as the citizens began to form a semi-circle at the end of the drawbridge. He raised his arms and motioned for them to quiet down and he unrolled the piece of paper Alanso had given him.

"Citizens of Hollyport, welcome!" He spoke with practiced ease and natural charisma. Although the king was an annoying and self-centered man, Alanso begrudgingly admired his ability to influence people with just the sound of his calming, reassuring voice.

The king continued, "I welcome you to Inner Earth! I am sure this is all quite overwhelming, but I assure you, we will do everything within our power to make you feel at home. Of course, after you have seen what this magical place has to offer if anyone wishes to return home they may do so of their own free will, but first please see what this place has to offer before making your decision." The king took a paint brush and bottle of paint out of the pocket of his robe and dipped the brush in. He began to paint on the wall, and when he was done, he splashed it with some of the special ingredient that made the magic happen. There was a loud popping sound and just like that, an umbrella appeared. The king smiled and handed it to a boy in the front row.

"Here you go, kid. In case it rains," they mayor said with a chuckle and his usual charming smile.

The boy smiled up at the king and then turned to his parents and tugged at their sleeves. "That was amazing! I want to live here. Please, can we? Can we?" The boy pulled at his parent's shirt sleeves, standing on tip-toes in excitement.

There was excited murmuring throughout the crowd. The king put the brush away and held up his hand and waited, once again, for quiet. "That is but a taste of what is possible. Imagine the world we could create here. All of you will be taught how to use this art we call Wizartry if you chose to stay."

The king had reached the end of the speech and turned towards Alanso.

Alanso stepped forward and did his best to put on a friendly smile. "I am Alanso, head of the Wizartry council. It is an honor to have you here at the Wizartry palace. There are enough rooms here for everyone. In the morning we will teach everyone some basic Wizartry and by the end of the day, you can make a decision about staying. Please, come on in." He beckoned them inside.

The crowd began to move forward through the gates in eager anticipation of what was to come. Rita stepped through the crowd and approached the king and Alanso.

"Good speech. Just don't forget who is in charge here," she reminded them. She kept her eyes locked on Alanso and then shifted her hard gaze to the king. With a grunt she pushed past them and followed the line into the palace.

\* \* \*

The citizens of Hollyport gathered in the palace courtyard. They milled about anxiously, excited murmurs spreading throughout the crowd.

Back in his room the king watched through the tower window each time he passed it as he paced back-and-forth, hands crossed behind his back. "Must we wait so long?" His spacious bedroom gave a clear view of the palace courtyard on one side and the other side of the room provided a magnificent view of the palace gardens and the forest beyond.

Alanso waited patiently behind the king, a knowing smirk on his face. "A king must let his subjects wait. He must let them know who is in charge."

"But they aren't my subjects yet. They haven't decided to stay yet," the king protested, edging away from the window as one in the crowd looked upward.

"They will be soon enough," Alanso said.

"How can you be so sure?" The king asked.

Alanso shrugged. "No one has left yet, and once they see what Wizartry has to offer, I doubt they will give up a chance like that. Besides..." he held up his finger for emphasis. "All we have to do is make sure the majority of people stay."

"What do you mean, 'make sure,'" the king asked, struggling to adjust the too small crown on his head to a more comfortable position, and failing.

"If most people decide to stay, it is very unlikely that more than a handful will want to return to Hollyport to live by themselves," Alanso explained. "Social pressure will make it hard for anyone to go against an entire town's wishes.

"That's a good point. I bet you are right!" The king peeked out the window again a little more enthusiastically.

"Of course I'm right," Alanso stated. "Stick with my advice and you will be a powerful king. Powerful beyond anything you have ever dreamed about."

The king clapped excitedly, just one more habit in a long list of habits that Alanso found annoying. How much longer would he have to put up with this moron? If it were up to him, Alanso would have gotten rid of the mayor a long time ago. Unfortunately, he had a lot of influence over the citizens of Hollyport. The townsfolk would never listen to someone like Alanso, but they would listen to someone they already respected and admired.

Alonso sat there debating with himself about whether or not to simply push the mayor out of the window and be done with him. He had just about convinced himself that the grief that Rita would put him through would probably be more annoying than the mayor was when the wooden doors to the bedroom swung open with a loud creak. Rita stepped through the doorway and stopped. "Are you two planning on talking all day and admiring the view, or do we want to organize the hundreds of people waiting outside?"

"Alanso was saying to..." The king started.

Alanso cut him off. "I was saying that we should hurry up. We were just planning on coming down."

Rita looked from Alanso to the king and then straight back to Alanso. "Good, because climbing these tower steps is not my idea of fun. I will have to have someone draw an elevator. There will be many changes in the upcoming weeks. I have business to attend to outside of town, but I expect you to be down there making sure everything is running smoothly while I am gone." She turned and left without waiting for a reply.

When she was gone, the king gave Alanso a quizzical look. "I thought you said we were supposed to wait?"

Alanso waived his hand dismissively. "Rita is always in a rush. She does not understand politics like you and I do."

The king nodded. "It is good that you will be my Wizartry Council advisor." He gave Alanso a beaming smile and placed his meaty hands on Alanso's shoulders. "You are a good man," he said. Alanso tried not to cringe under the uncomfortable grip. The king began to walk toward the doors.

"Where are you going?" Alanso asked.

"What do you mean? Rita just said to hurry up and you yourself said to..."

"Don't listen to her." Alanso yelled, much louder than he had intended. "We wait until the anticipation grows and the people know who is in charge."

"How long?"

"Until I say so," replied Alanso.

\* \* \*

Doodles Lanhorn walked the empty streets of Hollyport. The town was eerily quiet, the citizens all gone to Inner Earth. Laura walked quietly by his side, lost in her own thoughts. Doodles was thankful to have her company during this confusing and overwhelming time. They walked aimlessly, in silence, for a while, through the deserted streets, lost in their thoughts.

"We need to go get Darren and Riddley. We need to find my family and the council," Doodles finally said, breaking the silence.

Laura stopped abruptly and Doodles turned to look at her. "What about my family Doodles? Everyone is gone. It's not just about your family now."

"I'm sorry Laura. You're right. We'll find everyone and get them back. Everything will work out. I promise." Doodles wasn't sure of his own words but hoped that it sounded convincing enough to Laura. He didn't want her to be scared.

"I wish I could believe that," she said. This comment surprised Doodles as she was usually the optimistic and confident one in the group of friends. Laura continued, "I don't know if we will find everyone, and even if we do, things will never be the same. By now Rita has shown them everything about Wizartry. No one will want to come back to their old lives when they can have magic. It's too late."

Doodles opened his mouth to respond, to say something to give his friend hope, but nothing came out. What could he say if he didn't believe it himself?

"Doodles! Laura! Over here!" a familiar voice called out.

Doodles and Laura turned to see Riddley and Darren running towards them.

"Thank goodness we found you," Darren said as they approached. "We were worried sick."

"Riddley... We failed," Doodles said. "Rita brought everyone into Inner Earth. We tried to stop them in time." Doodles kept his head down, ashamed to look into Riddley's eyes. When Riddley didn't respond, Doodles looked up.

Riddley smiled. "You haven't failed, not yet. It's not too late."

"What do you mean? Everyone is gone. They know about Wizartry. The secret is out." Doodles clenched his fist. "And I failed the second test. I have no idea where my family is! Nothing had worked out."

Riddley shook his head and then adjusted his Wizartry hat as it nearly fell off of his head. "First of all, you didn't fail your second test. I never said you had to complete it right away. I am sure you will find them. And secondly..." He pulled his grey mustache thoughtfully.

"Riddley?" Doodles prompted.

"What?"" Riddley asked.

"Your second point?" Doodles exclaimed as patiently as he could manage under the circumstances. Sometimes getting information out of Riddley was like pulling teeth.

"Oh, yes. Secondly, it has only been one day since the secrets of Inner Earth and Wizartry were revealed to the citizens of Hollyport," Riddley stated.

"So?" Doodled asked. "What does how long they have known about it matter?"

"I probably shouldn't be sharing this," Riddley said. "But under the circumstances, I will make an exception. The council members have a secret relic that has been passed down since the council was founded. It has only been used a few times when emergency measures were needed in order to protect our world. And this certainly constitutes as an emergency."

"What is it?" Doodles asked.

"We don't know how it works exactly, but when used, it erases the memory of the last couple of days of anyone within a certain proximity of the palace," Riddley explained.

"That doesn't sound safe," Laura said. "I don't know if I want that used on my parents."

"It has been used several times before and everyone was fine," Riddley said. "Do you remember your history lessons on how the ancient pyramids were built? All false. Some Wizart thought it would be fun to paint giant structures, structures that were impossible to build with such complexity at the time. Even today, with all of the machinery and technology we have at our disposal, we would still be unable to do it. The council had to cover it up and make up some story about how they were built. Same thing with Stonehenge. You think people had the technology back then to carry those colossal stones from miles and miles away and stand them up with such precision? Ha! That's why we have to keep careful control, so that people don't draw whatever they want, where and whenever they want to."

"I still don't know..." Laura said.

Riddley shrugged. "What other choice do we have? Besides, I don't even know if we can gather everyone in one place. It's not exactly a full proof plan, but it's the best and only plan we have." Riddley pointed to the empty town. "Imagine if millions of people ran around drawing whatever they wanted. It would be utter chaos."

Laura sighed. "I understand. I just wish there was another way."

Riddley nodded. "Trust me, I wish there was another way too, but there isn't."

Doodles spoke up. "We still don't know where the council or my family is being held. They could be anywhere in Hollyport, Inner Earth, or anywhere in the world by now for that matter."

Darren looked around, spinning in a full circle. "Well, at least the town is empty. It will be easier to spot people and we can go anywhere we want." Doodles knew Darren was trying to sound hopeful, but the prospect of a completely empty town to explore was a daunting task. The council and his family could be anywhere. There just wasn't enough time or people to cover the entire town.

"We need to narrow our search. Otherwise we won't find them in time. Think guys. Is there anything you remember that was suspicious?" Doodles asked.

They all looked at each other, blank expressions on their faces. All of a sudden, Laura's face lit up. "The police station! The woman there tricked us into a cell. Your family could have been tricked the same way. They may be in another cell!"

Riddley added, "And if they took their paint brushes away from them, they wouldn't be able to paint their way out of the cell bars. That has to be the place! Right under our noses the whole time! Good work Laura! To the police station then!" He took off down the street, holding onto his hat as he ran to keep it from flying off of his head. Doodles was impressed that a man of his age could run so fast. Doodles looked to his friends and they took off after Riddley.

\* \* \*

The citizens of Hollyport gathered around in the palace courtyard. The king walked among them, giving a word of encouragement here, a compliment there, and smiling all the while.

Hundreds of easels were set up with canvases, paint and the special ingredient. The townsfolk painted excitedly, testing the limits of their newly discovered powers. Even the children stayed relatively still, taking in the artwork coming to life before them, their eyes wide with excitement and overwhelming curiosity.

Not a single person had protested or shown signs of wanting to leave yet. Alanso smiled at this fact. This was working out smoother than he could have ever thought possible. Rita would have to be dealt with soon but not just yet. He needed her help if things took a turn for the worst. He had to wait until everything was settled and then make his move.

Just as he finished this thought a great booming voice sounded from outside the palace walls. The walls shook, the ground trembled, and birds flew up into the air, startled. Children ran to their parents and hid behind them shaking.

"Your true king has returned!" The voice called out.

There was a moment of silence. The townsfolk looked around confused, trying to find the source of the voice. They then turned their eyes to the king. He in turn turned to Alanso who pointed to the ramparts along the palace walls.

"To the walls. Let us go and greet this visitor," said the king, starting to feel in charge. Alanso did not like where this was going. Who could possibly have such a commanding voice that the very walls would tremble? Why was this newcomer claiming to be a king? And why was the mayor starting to sound so kingly? Alanso did not like this turn of events. Just when things were finally coming together as he had planned.

"Hurry now. Move aside!" The king said as he tried to take command of the situation and pushed past the people now lining the walls. They pushed and pressed to get a better view. Alanso squeezed between them to get to the king's side.

"Who is that?" The king asked Alanso.

Alanso didn't know how to respond. It was a man, but almost too tall to be a man. He had to be at least nine feet tall. His body was covered from head to toe in blue paint or tattoos of some sort. If this was a man, he was the tallest man he had ever seen. "I don't know who that is," Alanso finally admitted.

The giant man held up one hand and the crowd of people along the walls quieted. It was so quiet that Alanso could swear he could hear his own heartbeat. Every second that went by was agonizingly full of tension.

"I am Loric," the stranger finally said after letting the tension build. The man then shouted, "I am your true and only king!" He began to raise his fists into the air and made guttural sounds. The sounds, already unnaturally loud, grew louder and louder until the people along the walls had to cover their ears.

"I have been waiting for my people to begin their return. Open the doors so that your king may enter!" Loric took a few steps forward and waited.

"What does he mean he is the king? I thought you said I would be king?" The mayor stammered, gripping Alanso's sleeve. The mayor had a panicked look in his eyes and after seeing the giant at the entrance to the palace, Alanso didn't feel much better himself.

"You are the king. This is some imposter. We won't open the gates. Eventually he will go away. The walls are too high for him to climb even if he is a giant," Alanso said and hoped he was right. Something about Loric made the hairs on the back of his neck stand up. He had the distinct feeling that this was a dangerous man. There was little doubt about that. Rita pushed through the crowd to join them. "This is someone we will not let in, "she said.

Alanso nodded. "For once, I couldn't agree with you more."

Loric began to grow impatient when he realized no one was moving to follow his order. "You have disappointed me! You leave me no choice but to come inside on my own!"

"Don't worry," Alanso said with a confident smile. "This intruder will not be able to get into the gates. They are not only sturdy, but are protected by ancient Wizartry magic. Even if this giant can use Wizartry, the outer walls are impervious to doors being drawn."

Loric held up his hands and began to wave them around. The tattoos on his body glowed brilliantly blue, illuminating the area around him.

"What is he doing?" Alanso asked in a nervous whisper. His confident smile began to fade. The crowd murmured and stood about uncertainly.

Rita pointed. "It can't be! I thought Doodles was the only one that could do that!" Sure enough, Loric had created something with his just his hands. Alanso gulped. Loric had drawn a large battering ram. The walls could protect against Wizartry, but a giant with a battering ram might be another story.

# Chapter 15

Hollyport's streets and sidewalks were never really crowded, but with no one there it was like walking through an abandoned movie set. There were cars left in the middle of the street with their doors still open. Closed signs hung in storefront windows. Birds ate freely the scraps of food in front of restaurants with no one to shoo them away.

A sudden gust of wind knocked a few magazines from a stand onto the sidewalk. Doodles stopped himself halfway down to pick them up. There was no need to pick them up if there weren't any townsfolk. His mother had always told him that being a good person was doing the right thing even if no one was around to see it. Clearly no one was around, but the priority of saving lives in a short time period outweighed picking up trash. Doodles missed his family. He needed them back more than ever.

The police station was the only building that didn't look completely abandoned. There were lights on through the windows, and several shapes walked back and forth inside.

"Do we just walk right inside?" Darren asked uncertainly.

Doodles looked to Riddley and laughed despite the situation they were in. Riddley gave a look to Doodles and a nod that Doodles knew all too well.

"Riddley will distract them while we go in and rescue every-one," Doodles explained. "If there is one person for the distrac-tion job, it's Riddley."

Riddley gave a wide smile and shooed them to the side. "Off with you then. Go inside once the fireworks go off." He chuckled as he began to paint.

Doodles and his friends hurried to the side to duck behind a taxi cab. Doodles couldn't help smile when he looked at his friends. They had come with him, trusted him with their safety to help him even though he hid things, important things from them, from the start. They had been with him through everything. They were real and true friends. He didn't think he could have made it this far without them. They believed in him even when he didn't believe in himself.

Riddley was done painting and covered his ears with his hands. The fireworks began soon after. He had gone somewhat overboard on the fireworks as they shot off in every direction down the street, some even hitting the taxi cab the three friends were hiding behind. Almost too predictably, three officers exited the front door of the station and headed toward Riddley. Riddley turned and ran, the three officers pursuing him on foot.

"Let's go!" Doodles urged.

"But what about Riddley?" Darren asked.

Doodles headed to the front saying, "trust me, he'll lose them when he wants to. It's only a matter of how long he can stall before they realize they've been duped."

They hurried up the steps; through the front door and down the hallway until they located the cells. In the third cell they found the council and Doodles' family.

* * *

Loric charged, his great muscles tensing as he lumbered forward with the battering ram. The blue tattoos on his body glowed brightly with unearthly light. The Hollyport citizens gasped in fear as Loric crashed full speed into the palace gate. The whole building seemed to shake to its very foundation. The gate gave a loud moan, splinters of wood flying off in all directions, but it held.

He emitted a thunderous laugh and picked up the battering ram again. "One more should do it," Loric said in a matter of fact tone. I'm in no rush."

He began to walk back to give himself more running room. "See you all on the inside in a minute," he said with a confident grin.

From up on the walls the people began to panic. Some of the citizens didn't know if they wanted to be there anymore. Inner Earth no longer seemed like an enchanting and beautiful place. The spell and allure Inner Earth normally casts over newcomers was wearing off quickly.

"Let us out of here, we want to go back home!" One man yelled. He began to push forward until Rita raised her voice.

"The only thing stopping that lunatic out there is these walls. I will find a way to deal with him," she yelled vehemently.

The man wanted to continue his protest, but Rita glared at him, raising her paint brush as if daring him to make another step forward. Reluctantly, the man stood still.

"Walk with me Alanso. Now!" Rita commanded.

The two of them broke apart from the crowd and walked a way down the ramparts.

"Do we have a plan?" Alanso asked.

"This stranger is unnaturally strong and fast on top of possessing Doodles' brushless painting powers. The only weakness I can see is that he is overconfident. Whoever this Loric really is, he doesn't think any of us are a match for him and that will be his downfall."

"He is overconfident because he is all of those things you say. And it's true that no one here can take him on. So how does knowing he is confident help us?" Alanso gave a nervous look toward Loric down below, as he prepared to charge the door again. The giant was just about at his new starting point further back. In another minute he would be charging the gate for another, possibly final blow.

"Must I do everything around here?" Rita sighed and began to paint. A long rope appeared in her hands. She tied it around one of the columns and began to descend the wall, rappelling down by pushing with her legs off of the side of the wall.

When she reached the ground she ran towards Loric. From where he was standing, Alanso thought it was like watching an ant charging a lion. He chuckled. Maybe he would be getting rid of Rita sooner than he had anticipated. She was reckless. As she neared Loric, Alanso tensed, anticipating that Loric would squash her like a bug. Instead, and much to Alanso's dismay, it appeared that they were having a conversation.

"If you are here to surrender, then kneel. If you are here to fight me then you insult me," Loric said. He flicked the battering ram to the side like a discarded toothpick and it crashed into the earth with such tremendous force that a cloud of dust rose into the air. For the first time Alanso thought, just for a second, that he saw a look of fear flash in Rita's eyes, but her face quickly returned to its normal expression of grim determination. She locked eyes with Loric and neither lowered their gaze.

"I am here to offer you a challenge," Rita replied.

"And what challenge would that be?" Loric asked, mildly amused. Here was a tiny woman daring to stand before him with a challenge.

"There is someone I believe is stronger than you. He is the rightful king of Inner Earth."

Loric's fist clenched. "There is no one stronger than me! I have been waiting for the time when my people would return and I would reclaim Inner Earth. I was here when Inner Earth first was created, I lost my strength when so many of my devoted followers were driven away but they are returning and my strength is returning with them!"

Rita laughed. "You are nothing compared to this new one, you can trust me on that."

"What is his name? I demand to know who this person is. Where is he? Let him show his face to me." Loric said through clenched teeth, his face turning red with anger.

"Doodles. His name is Doodles and he is coming this way. Face him and the winner can claim Inner Earth as his kingdom." Rita knew he had him then.

"I will crush this Doodles and then I will take my place as king."

Rita did not doubt Loric but she smiled. When you find yourself between a rock and a hard place, simply step out of the way and let the rock smash into the hard place.

# Chapter 16

**D**oodles, Riddley, Darren, Laura, and Boogley waved goodbye to Doodles' family and the council members. After rescuing them, Doodles realized they were too exhausted from their ordeal to be of any help and needed rest more than anything. They left them in a safe house, one Riddley assured them only he knew about. Their goodbyes were quick, yet heartfelt. Doodles was so happy to know they were safe, but he knew he still had a long road ahead of him. The entire town and Inner Earth still needed to be saved.

With the council and his family safe, the group set off toward Inner Earth. They moved in silence, each one lost in his or her own thoughts. These were troubling times for all of them. When they were finally back in Inner Earth, Laura tapped Doodles on the shoulder.

"Doodles, I need you to trust me with something," Laura said.

"Is everything okay?" Doodles asked. She had sounded so serious.

Laura ignored his question. "I need you to tell me you trust me."

"Of course I trust you, Laura. You're my best friend," Doodles said.

"Good. Then I need you to continue on without me. I remember something you told me last time you were here in Inner

Earth. If what I have planned works, it may just be the thing that saves us. We don't have time for all of us to go so I need you to keep on your path," Laura said.

Doodles stared at her in disbelief. "I trust you..." he said, knowing anything else he might say would be of no use. When Laura put her mind to something, there was no turning her back.

"Good. We both better hurry then," she said, and in a moment she was off, leaving Doodles and the others with a lot of questions and worry.

* * *

Doodles, Darren, Boogley, and Riddley approached the palace. From this distance, Doodles could spot hundreds of people lining the walls. Darren tried to find Laura's parents in the sea of faces, but from this distance it was impossible. They were tired from all of the running and walking they had done recently and the palace seemed so far away still. This was the first time that Darren had seen the palace and it was even more amazing than Doodles' recount of his last adventure made it out to be. With its high walls and beautifully designed gate and towers, it stood as a testament to not only the beauty of Inner Earth, but to the creativity and skill that Wizartry could create. They stood for a few minutes in awe until the palace faded into the background as a giant of a man neared.

The giant stopped a few yards from them, his booming voice washing over them with clear power and confidence. "Who among you is Doodles?"

Doodles gulped. "I am," he said, hoping this was a friend, but somehow, Doodles doubted it. His voice had come out like a squeak. This wasn't just some bully at his school. This giant of a man looked almost exactly like the statue they had discovered in the forest earlier.

The giant looked him over a few times and laughed. "I am Loric, the once and future king of all Inner Earth." When Loric spoke, a flashback of the writing on the base of the statue came into Doodles' mind. It was not mere coincidence that Loric not only looked exactly like the statue, but also spoke the words on it.

Doodles looked to Riddley for guidance. Riddley seemed just as troubled. Doodles wished Laura was here. She would know what to do, or at least come up with some sort of plan of action.

"Hello, Loric," Doodles responded having no idea how to respond to that statement.

Loric leaned forward menacingly as he towered over Doodles, blocking the sunlight and casting a dark shadow over him. "You will challenge me to a duel. When I crush you, all will bow to me," Loric commanded.

Riddley placed his hand on Doodles' shoulder. "The blue markings. I have only read about them in ancient Wizartry history books. He is an ancient Wizart. Their powers have not been seen since... well since well before my time. You can't beat him. Talk your way out of it," Riddley whispered.

Doodles pointed to the palace. "It is such a big palace."

Loric's face grew stern. "You are stalling."

Doodles froze with fear. Riddley was usually the one who told him he could accomplish anything if he put his mind to it, but the fact that Riddley told him he could not win made Doodles more scared than the giant before him. None of them could face this man.

"Where did you come from?" Doodles asked.

"No more words," Loric commanded. He picked up the battering ram and like a pencil, he used it to carve a large circle in the sand. "No one leaves this circle until one of us is victorious."

Loric motioned for Doodles to enter the circle. He stretched his powerful arms out and then cracked his knuckles in anticipation.

Doodles looked up at Loric and then to his friends. This was going from bad to worse. Doodles was sure he would never leave that circle once he entered it. There had to be another way. Even if he magically found a way to deal with Loric, Doodles still had to face Alanso, Rita, and the mayor. Doodles wiped sweat from his brow. Sometimes everything just seemed like too much to handle by himself. This was one of those times.

As if she had read his mind, Laura's voice called out from behind him, "Figured you could use the help of some more friends!"

Doodles turned. There, just coming out of the forest leading to the palace were hundreds of elderly men and women. All of them carried paint brushes. Although some of them walked unsteadily, these were Wizarts. They held their heads high; each one sporting an elaborate Wizartry hat, a symbol of their power and heritage.

Laura ran over and gave Doodles a hug. "I remembered you told me about Inner Earth having a town full of retired Wizarts. I remembered where you said the town was located. As soon as they heard you were in trouble they began to march. We will always have your back, Doodles." She gave him a gentle kiss on the cheek and he blushed.

Doodles looked over at the men and woman now standing behind him. "You can't beat us all," Doodles said to Loric. Loric bellowed with rage, howling into the air with his arms shaking toward the heavens. The Wizarts held their line. Loric looked them over, weighing his chances. For a moment, Doodles thought Loric would charge all of them.

Darren surprised Doodles and Laura by stepping forward. He walked right up to the giant and looked up at him. "I have always been scared," he started. Loric gave him a puzzled look, clearly surprised someone so small and insignificant in his mind would dare to speak to him so close. "Every step of this adventure I wanted to turn back. But I didn't. And do you know why? Because of them," Darren pointed back to Doodles and Laura and all the rest of the Wizarts. "I don't need to be scared any more with so many wonderful friends. But you... you are by yourself, and that must be scarier than anything I have ever faced."

There was a great moment of silence. Doodles could not have been more proud of his friend. Loric gave one last look of defiance and then, with a grunt, Loric began to walk away, back toward the forests. "This is not the last you will see of me," he warned.

The Wizarts cheered as one. Doodles gave his friends a thankful look and they all marched toward the palace. Doodles couldn't help looking over his shoulder in case Loric came charging back.

"Everyone has to be gathered in one place for the orb to work," Riddley said as they neared the gates. "We have more than enough Wizarts to deal with Rita and her minions if they try and stop us now."

Doodles could not believe how things had turned out. Because of his friends and the Wizartry community coming together, they had saved the day! Not only would his family be safe, but Doodles had passed the second Wizartry test and was one test away from being a Wizart, with all of the privileges and honor that came with it.

The palace gates were nearly ripped apart from Loric's battering ram but they still opened as the group approached. Laura's father and mother were the first ones to run out and embrace her. The rest of the Hollyport citizens were soon to follow. Doodles scanned their faces. There was no sign of Alazo, Rita, or the mayor. They must have slipped away when they saw the Wizarts approaching.

"Gather around!" Riddley yelled out. He then turned to Doodles." After I use this, there will only be a short amount of time to get them back to Hollyport. They will be in a daze and confused for quite some time when they come to. We must make sure we get them all out of Inner Earth before it wears off."

Doodles nodded his understanding. The citizens of Hollyport gathered together around Riddley. Doodles imagined they must still be in shock from seeing all of Inner Earth and Wizartry, the good and the bad of it, all at once. Doodles remembered his first time here. It had been awesome but overwhelming and he had known that he would be facing danger.

Riddley took the globe out of a pouch at his side. Doodles was taken aback by how beautiful it was. It seemed ancient, yet powerful. The orb was a smooth, clear crystal which rested on an intricately carved golden handle. Rubies and sapphires dotted the handle's exterior, sparkling brightly in the sun. A golden serpent curled around the handle and up around the circumference of the crystal globe, a fiery red, forked tongue stuck out.

Riddley addressed the townsfolk, "Hello everyone! Gather around now, no need to be shy. I want to show all of you something that will only take a minute of your time." He held the globe into the air and muttered something that Doodles couldn't understand. A faint wisp of smoke appeared around the globe, coming forth in steady plumes from the golden serpent's nostrils, swirling clockwise in slow waves, tendrils of blue smoke starting to spread out, enveloping the awestruck crowd. It spread further and further out until every last citizen of Hollyport was inside of the cloud of fog.

Doodles hoped this would work. If it didn't, nothing would ever be the same in Hollyport. The whole world would change and the sanctity of Inner Earth would be in jeopardy.

There was a bright flash. The fog dissipated as quickly as it had come. The townsfolk of Hollyport stared ahead with blank stares.

Riddley placed the orb back into his pouch.

"Well, did it work?" Doodles asked.

He looked around and shrugged. "I've never personally used it, but it looks like it worked. We only have a few hours before they come to and we must have them back by then or it will make it much harder to explain. They will be disoriented but will be able to walk with prompting. Lead all of them back to Hollyport. Boogley and I have to remain behind in Inner Earth to help finishing putting things right and to organize groups to look for Alanso, Rita and the mayor. They couldn't have gotten too far away."

Doodles nodded. He looked to Laura and Darren.

"What are we waiting for?" Laura asked. "Let's do this."

* * *

Doodles' mother and father embraced him in a tight hug. He had never missed them so much. His father beamed down on him with pride and his mother's eyes were teary.

"We are so proud of you," Mr. Lanhorn said. He ruffled Doodles' hair.

"We never had a doubt you would save us," his mother said. She wiped away a tear. "I'm so sorry you had to go through all of that alone."

Doodles smiled. "I didn't have to go through it alone. I had my friends with me, and there is nothing stronger than the power of friendship. I've learned that on this journey."

Uncle Roger and Aunt Martha took this as their turn to give him a hug. Their hugs usually lasted way too long and was way too hard. This time was no exception. He gasped for air toward the end.

"You are well on your way to joining the Wizarts," Uncle Roger said.

"One last test," Aunt Martha said.

"For now, I think we should all take it easy. It's been a long week," Doodles said.

They all shared a well-deserved laugh.

\* \* \*

"Pass the salt," Laura's father asked Doodles. Doodles smiled and handed him the salt shaker.

"Thank you again for having me over for dinner," Doodles said. He looked over to Laura who in turn smiled and winked at him.

"Our pleasure," Laura's mother said. She passed Doodles a basket of freshly baked bread. "Don't be shy now. Take as much as you want."

Doodles grabbed one piece of bread and put it on his plate. "You always cook the best meals."

Laura's mother smiled. "Laura is lucky to have you as a friend, Doodles. Such a well-mannered and kind boy."

"Actually," Doodles said. "I am lucky to have someone like Laura as a friend in my life." He looked over to her and they shared a knowing look. After all they had been through, the two of them would share a bond that could never be broken. Hollyport was saved. The townsfolk had no memory of what had happened and no idea about the existence of Wizartry. For a while things had spiraled out of control in the wrong direction. Without his friends, it could have ended badly. Thankfully, things had returned to normal… for now.

The End

# About the Author

**R**ussell D. Bernstein was born and raised in Miami, Florida. He currently resides in Orange, Connecticut with his family. Russell has a Masters in Organizational Leadership and has extensive experience in the healthcare field. Russell has used those experiences as background for writing and his talks at schools. For more on Russell, go to his main website: www.bullytalks.com

Made in the USA
San Bernardino, CA
04 September 2016